An Empty Sky

by
frank drury

Printed by CREATESPACE

ISBN: 1449974902
ISBN-13: 9781449974909
www.frankdrury.com

*Dedicated to my loving wife Lisa
and my children Jackson, Jenna,
Dana, and Taylor*

CHAPTER I

It was a cloudy Saturday morning back in August 1985 at Stan's Marina in Ocean City, Maryland, where he had come to meet the others. He felt the excitement in the air as they all loaded the 42 ft. Bertram Cruiser for a weekend at sea. Mike could tell the other guys did this on a regular basis when he saw their fishing gear. The skipper's name was Toby, a big man, fat yet muscular, and he approached Mike with a cooler full of beer. In a very loud voice he told Mike to stow the beer below.

It was about noon when the boat entered the rough waters of the Atlantic. Toby set their course for a point about ten nautical miles out from Virginia Beach. There was an overcast sky, darker in some areas than others, and a wind that seemed to pick up in strength the farther out they traveled.

At this point, Hurricane David was still about four hundred miles southeast of Myrtle Beach, South Carolina. Mike mentioned the storm to Toby's two friends, trying to get some kind of confirmation back that there was nothing to worry about. Toby's two pals, Ben and Osborn, began telling stories about other storms they had been through. Ben and Osborn were real estate developers and had been buddies since childhood. They had gone through the Vietnam War together, both in the Army. Watching Ben and Osborn slug down beers as the waves grew bigger gave Mike an uneasy feeling, especially in his stomach.

Mike Chandler was thirty-two years old, although he looked a lot younger at first glance. His hair was light brown, almost blond, and cut short. His eyes were deep blue in color, even without contact lenses, and when he wore the lenses the color became even more cobalt. He was tall and in very good physical condition. He didn't have much of a tan, even after being in the sun all summer. His complexion had more of a burnt and ruddy appearance.

As a boy his father had taken him fishing on a fairly regular basis, mostly in and around the creeks and tributaries of the Chesapeake Bay because he would get seasick fishing in the ocean. After his father died when Mike was nineteen, he rarely went fishing at all. He completely threw himself into his schoolwork and graduated at twenty-seven with a doctorate in Clinical Psychology.

When he was invited by Toby to go deep sea fishing, he jumped at the chance.

They cut the engines at sundown, although the overcast sky made it difficult to tell how much more daylight was left. Toby brought some steaks up from below and told Mike to get a fire going in the grill he had set up on deck. The rocky motion of the boat had forced Toby to anchor the legs of the grill heavily with sandbags. There seemed to be a surreal quality to the whole picture as Mike watched Toby climb up the steps from the cabin carrying two large sirloin steaks in one hand and a bottle of bourbon in the other. The grill was a gas grill and Mike got it started easily while Ben and Osborn joined Toby in a couple of pulls from the bottle of Old Fitzgerald.

After eating their dinner, Ben and Osborn retired to the cabin. Ben, to "take a dump," and Osborn, to "bunk down for awhile." Toby began to show Mike how to set the gear up for night fishing. The sea had calmed a bit and it wasn't long before Mike and Toby were both fishing, silently enjoying the cool night air.

Nothing was said between the two of them for about fifteen minutes, until Ben returned from the cabin with a great deal of noise. The foul odor of his business from below followed him right up the steps.

"Jesus Christ, Ben!" Toby exclaimed. "And I suppose Osborn is sound asleep down there?"

"Either passed out or knocked out, one or the other." Ben belched and walked over to the cooler for another beer. "Anything hittin'?"

"Nothing yet, boy, nothing yet." Toby liked to call Ben "boy" simply because he knew it pissed him off.

"Fuck you, Toby." Ben climbed up towards the bow of the boat and sat down, leaning up against the railing for support.

It was silent for awhile before Mike brought it up again. "So Toby, how soon will David get up this way if he doesn't hit the coast down south?"

"You still thinking about that storm? She's three hundred miles away!"

"It's a 'he' Toby, and the way I figure it at twenty miles per hour he could be real close by tomorrow afternoon," Mike responded.

"Hey Ben, you worried about the storm?" Toby shouted. There was no response. Ben had passed out as well up on the bow.

"Pussy," Toby muttered back towards Ben, after getting no reply.

"It just seems to me..." Mike began, "I mean to be out here under these circumstances, is that kind of, I don't know, not real safe?"

"Not a thing to worry about." Toby's voice grew quieter as he muttered something else to himself, inaudible to Mike.

Mike sat dreamily gazing out over the choppy surface of the water that stretched for miles into the horizon. The moon could not be seen, yet the light from it illuminated the eerie cloud cover. Mike began to think about the fish in the water below, the depth of the water, and even what it might look like hundreds of feet below on the floor of the ocean. After about an hour had passed, Toby muttered, "Fuck it!" to himself and went below to get some sleep. Mike was so lost in thought he barely heard him leave.

Mike closed his eyes and held the rod loosely in his hands. He filled his mind with the image of a turn-of-the-century whaler's boat, about twenty-five feet in length, filled with a half dozen rough-looking oarsmen working at a frenetic pace to keep the small boat steady enough, yet still moving swiftly enough, for the lone harpooner to angrily hurl his crude, yet lethal, spear into the shiny black skin of the creature who had just surfaced for a breath of fresh air. Mike saw a twisted look of anger on the killer's face and a look of pleasure on the faces of the oarsmen, all except one, and Mike recognized the compassion on the face of this one sea-drenched whaler. He saw the pain that the man was feeling as the others around him encouraged each other on and Mike felt like he too had experienced that same pain before.

At this precise moment, the rod was nearly pulled out of Mike's hands and he was seeing only the open sea in front of him. As he set the drag a little looser he grimaced in a way very much like one of the less timid whalers of his mind's eye. He pulled the rod up in one swift motion to set the hook. Once done, the fight began. Mike's mind was intensely focused on first his hands, then the reel, then the line, then the rod, and finally the sea and his prey below.

He knew it was a big fish. This much had been established in the first few seconds, critical moments, after he had set the hook. Now it was simply a matter of working it in and not being too slow or too fast about it. The fish dived deep and the reel hummed relentlessly as the line raced away. Mike was unaware of Toby's presence behind him as he continued to focus only on the fish. He slowly let the rod ease down towards the horizon and quickly brought it back up again and it was then that he knew the fish was gone. He began to reel in the several hundred feet of line very slowly as Toby mumbled, "Tough fucking break!" before returning to his bunk below, half carrying Ben with him down the steps into the cabin. As Mike reeled in the line, it felt as though he was reeling in nothing, yet he saw the heavy, clear pale-green line move onto the reel in his lap and his hands continued to tremble even after the final wet strand of line slipped through the top guide of his rod and noiselessly flapped around the reel before coming to a rest in his lap.

He sat transfixed for a long while as though he were deep in thought, when actually he was only numb. He thought of the big fish below swimming furiously away from the boat with the hook set firmly in its jaw. After a few long, quiet minutes had passed, Mike placed the rod down on to the floor of the boat and stood up to stretch his muscles. It seemed like the wind had picked up and he realized the storm was getting closer.

It was sometime later that night, long after Mike had wrapped himself up in a damp down blanket and fallen asleep under a tarp in the stern of the boat, that the sudden impact of something hitting the side of the boat awoke all but one of the sleeping fishermen.

Mike was the first to see the catamaran, rather, a part of a catamaran that had struck them. It was only a few feet away from the boat. Toby and Osborn both joined him from below and all three of them stared in disbelief at the single blue and white pontoon about fifteen feet in length as it glistened in the light from the flashlight Toby held on it. It still had the net-like seating attached to its side and Osborn was the first to notice a body clinging tightly to its tattered rigging.

"What the fuck?" Osborn exclaimed.

Then Mike saw it too and yelled, "Someone hanging on there!"

Toby responded immediately as he threw open a storage compartment in the rear and pulled out a long rope and started shouting orders. "Throw this over the front. Osborn, get that hook, there, get it out." He was referring to a long aluminum pole in a rack along the inner side of the cruiser. "Hold it there," he shouted. "Mike, get the rope out there." The entire lower deck of the cruiser was a scene of frantic confusion, yet somehow they managed to get one end of the rope attached to part of the rigging on the catamaran.

Toby started the engine of the cruiser and slowly started to move it closer to the long bluish missile that lay alongside the Bertram in the rough water. He was able to move it just a few feet closer and Osborn was able to get one end of the pole wedged into a gap between the rigging and the cat. Mike watched as it edged closer to them and when it was only a few feet away he began to precariously reach out for something to hold on to. After several futile attempts to grab a rope hanging off the side of the boat he finally got it. He jumped into the water. He held tightly to the rope with one hand as he swam towards the lifeless body. It all happened so fast and when they finally got the girl's body on board, none of them said a thing at first. There she lay, soaking wet, semi-conscious, somewhat delirious, and shivering convulsively. Mike wrapped her up in the same down blanket he had been sleeping in moments before.

They moved her carefully into the cabin, disturbing the sleeping Ben as they turned on the light. Ben, who always looked as though he needed a shave, looked especially haggard as he woke up and scratched his head while staring at the girl. "Well I'll be a son of a bitch," he offered.

"Move off the bunk, son of a bitch," responded Toby. "Let's get her down here, fellas." They put her down on the bunk and Toby began to undress her. She appeared to be about seventeen or eighteen years old. Her long hair was wet and matted, dark red in color, and her face, though somewhat pallid, was beautiful.

"Wait a minute," Mike protested. "Don't you think we ought to leave her clothes…."

"Shut the fuck up," responded Toby as he hurriedly unfastened her shirt, quickly covering her breasts with a blanket as he moved her shirt off over her shoulders. He barked for another blanket as he wrapped her upper body snugly in the first one. He began to unfasten her wet jeans and turned to see the other three all staring down at her. In Mike's outstretched hand was another blanket. "Will you guys please stop gawking? Jesus Christ. Osborn, make some coffee. Ben, get that portable heater out from below." He grabbed the blanket and had her out of the wet jeans before any of the others got more than a glimpse at her trembling legs. She passed out and Toby gently wrapped the rest of her in the blanket. He then helped Ben with the heater. The temperature in the cabin was probably in the sixties but Toby wanted to make it much warmer for her. As he shuffled the others outside on to the deck he glanced back at her once more and thought of his own daughter, who was about the same age.

He quickly closed the cabin door and carried the coffee pot up the steps to the deck where the others were waiting. They were watching the cloud-covered night sky slowly become morning. There was a dim, hazy light on the horizon, slowly climbing upwards, illuminating the surface of the water as the sun began to rise.

II

Kevin Kepler walked along the windswept beach, straining his eyes to see a sign of some kind from the rough, pounding waves that roared into the ordinarily calm inlet at Fenwick Island, Delaware. The sky was dark gray and although it had not yet begun to rain, it was obviously going to start pouring very soon. The cloud cover was solid and visibility was limited to only a mile as Kevin stared out into the rolling swells. The wind slapped the brown lapel of his jacket up against the side of his somber, chiseled face, a face that said little about the forty-seven years of his life, yet also seemed to say something very specific at the same time.

His daughter, Virginia, had been missing since the day before when she and her boyfriend had set out on a quick sail to take advantage of the good winds the hurricane was bringing up from North Carolina. She and her boyfriend had gone out against Kevin's wishes and over twenty-four hours had now passed. He had been walking the beach since dawn, not so much thinking that he might find her, but more in an effort to remain composed. He knew the Coast Guard was looking for her and, more importantly, he knew two friends of his from his days as a Special Forces Major were also out looking for her in a helicopter. He preferred walking the beach to staying up at the house with Megan, his wife, and her father, as they listened for some radio message from the Coast Guard. His daughter, Virginia, was from his first wife, Liz, who had died over ten years ago.

A few seagulls glided aimlessly through the wind over the breaking waves and Kevin's mind grew closer to feeling what he needed to feel. A growing calm, a serenity that seemed to slowly come over him, growing in intensity, finally leaving him with the balance he desired and always seemed to obtain. He took great pride in his many achievements and it showed when he spoke of them in his own offhand sort of way, especially showing when he grinned like a little boy before his face would quickly take on a deeply serious expression.

Up in the main house, an expansive Cape-Cod that Kevin's family had built many years ago only a short distance from the water, Megan sat nervously entertaining her guests. Her father had driven down from Baltimore the night before and at seventy-five was still the energetic soul he had been for as long as she could remember, the same unknown scientist who, thirty years ago, had given the world a vaccine for polio just days after Salk had announced his own vaccine. Just as it had not discouraged him at all when he missed his chance at fame back then, it now seemed that he was equally unperturbed by what he called their current predicament. His balding head was splotched with liver spots and his wire-rimmed spectacles moved up and down on his nose when he talked in an animated fashion. One could easily picture him as a young man, which for somebody his age was extremely flattering. He spoke to his daughter as she stood up against the big bay window, staring down at Kevin on the beach below.

"Relax, Meg, What do you figure she went off and did? Anyway, I know she's all right, just fine, sitting somewhere right now having a cup of hot cocoa."

"Shut up, Dad." Megan was shorter on patience than she cared to be but that was just too bad. It was watching what it was doing to Kevin that hurt her so much. She loved Virginia like her own daughter but she loved Kevin more than life itself, and the pain she was feeling was overwhelming. "I'm sorry, Dad," she added softly.

She turned away from the window and walked over to where the old man was sitting. "I just can't handle this waiting, that's all. I just wish we knew something, you know?"

"That's okay, it's okay. Here. Sit with me." Her father made room for her in the chair beside him and held her tightly around the shoulders when she sat down next to him, gently rocking her back and forth as he stared out the window at the darkening sky.

Kevin's nephew, Jimmy, came bounding into the room with an arm full of firewood. "How about a fire?" Jimmy exclaimed as he noisily put the wood down, opened the screen, and began to place kindling on the grate.

"Make sure the flue is open, Jimmy," said his Grandpop.

"I know, Pop." He continued with the wood as he talked. "Don't you think Uncle Kevin's friends will find her?" Jimmy was thirteen and was in awe of his uncle. He loved it every time he got to come down from Baltimore for a visit.

"I hope so sweetie," replied Megan. She loved her sister's son like he was her own.

"I mean if she's still okay they'll find her, right?" Jimmy asked. For the first time, a look of serious concern was on his face.

"That's right. That's what we're praying for." She hugged her Dad and quickly stood up to move out of the room.

All of the rooms were made to feel warm and cozy by the dark, reddish-brown, Knotty Pine paneling that had been used when the house was first built. Wonderful landscapes, all originals, hung on the walls. The walls were also adorned with a valuable collection of firearms and weapons.

On the sofa sat Mr. & Mrs. Hollingsworth, friends of the family for years, since Kevin was a boy, and neighbors that had proven their loyalty and goodwill many times over the years. Kevin was especially fond of Mrs. Hollingsworth and a mother-son relationship had blossomed long ago. They had come over the night before upon first hearing about the situation from Jimmy, who had mentioned it in a casual manner, not fully knowing how serious it would soon become. Mrs. Hollingsworth had sensed immediately that it might be worth a visit. She was one of the few people who could bring laughter to Kevin's usually stoic face, and though she had not made him laugh last night she had certainly made him feel better.

Kevin sensed that something was wrong as he stared out into the ocean, he could not quite shake it even when he tried. With an inner calm haunted by a bad premonition he walked back up to the house.

He came in through the kitchen door at the side of the house and walked directly over to the phone. He started to dial a number and then he hung up the receiver. He walked into the back study where his radio equipment hummed and several red lamps were lit up at strategic places on the front of the transceiver. He began to place a radio call to his friends.

Mrs. Hollingsworth entered the room silently and walked up behind him, placing her hands on his shoulders without saying a word. Kevin extended his hand to one of hers as he continued the radio call.

III

The sun had been up for about an hour and Toby turned the boat back towards land, determined to get the girl back to Ocean City and then to the hospital faster than he figured the Coast Guard could do it. He knew the girl would be better off if she were kept warm and dry and allowed to sleep down below. He knew how the Coast Guard would handle it: helicopter, exposure to the elements again, a ride through high winds, possible delays. He knew he could be in Ocean City by ten o'clock and have an ambulance move her on to the hospital by eleven.

"Perhaps you should call the Coast Guard anyway, Toby. I mean, they're probably looking for her," Mike said quietly.

"Just let me handle it." Toby paused, his round, red face absorbing the pressure from the wind as they sped towards land. Ben and Osborn sat quietly on a bench and said nothing.

Below in the bunk, Virginia was dreaming, half-delirious. She was not aware of what was happening. She was dreaming of her horses. She was at her father's horse ranch in Northern Virginia and riderless horses were jumping in slow motion while she looked on from her seat on top of the old red tractor that stood outside the riding area. Her fiancé, Nathan, was with her and everything seemed quite normal until she realized his face had changed, had become the face of someone else, and then had changed back to his own again, and the riderless horses kept on running in a great circle as they jumped, as though they were creating an ethereal ballet with their motion. Then she was on the catamaran, it was raining and they were speeding along in the wind. They were smiling and they were laughing. Then she heard a voice and opened her eyes.

Mike was staring down at her and smiling, asking her, "How ya doing?"

"Who is this guy?" she thought to herself as she closed her eyes again and felt feverish, even nauseous.

She opened them again as she asked, "Who are you? Where am I?" She tried to sit up and he gently put his hands on her shoulders and eased her back down again.

"Relax, you're okay. Relax." Mike's voice was reassuring. "Feel like you could drink some coffee?"

"Sure. What happened?" She took the cup and held it with both hands. She looked around the cabin of the boat and realized that her clothes were hanging up on a peg by the door.

"You were wet," Mike was quick to offer, "very wet. And cold."

She began to feel lightheaded again and handed him the cup of coffee. "Who undressed me?"

Mike chuckled and answered, "Toby."

"Who?" She opened her eyes again.

"The Captain. Toby. He's up there." He motioned towards the steps.

"Oh," was her only response. After a moment she asked, "Where are we?"

"On our way to Ocean City."

"And what about the storm?"

"Oh it's still there, can't you tell?" He was referring to the rocky motion of the boat and the sound of the wind over the roar of the inboard.

"Yea." She puffed up her cheeks, exhaled, and took a deep breath before the coughing began. It came from deep inside her lungs and sounded awful. It was over in a few minutes.

"Doesn't sound real good, does it?" she commented.

Mike stood over her now as the cabin door opened and Toby entered. "We'll be there in about an hour. How you doin' hon?" He walked over to her and put his palm on her forehead. "Get her some aspirin, Mike." Without stopping, he continued speaking to her, "What's your name, Red?"

"Virginia. Virginia Kepler," she replied.

"What happened to you?" Toby asked with concern.

"I don't know. Something hit us." She thought about Nathan going under as his hand slid off the side of the catamaran only inches away from where she too had been holding on. She had been too weak to reach out for him and then he was gone. "I don't remember it all." She closed her eyes again and started to tremble.

"It's okay, hon, it's okay. Here, take these." Toby handed her the aspirin and a red plastic cup half full of water.

"Have you called the Coast Guard? I'm sure my father is looking for me." Her dark brown eyes glistened in the light of the lamp near the bunk and Toby thought again of his own daughter.

"No, I figured we'd have you there sooner than they would."

"I think you ought to call anyway. My dad will be waiting, you know, for the call."

"Yea, I know. I'll call right now," Toby assured her as he covered her shoulders with the blanket before standing up to place the call.

IV

Kevin heard the call to the Coast Guard from Toby and a smile came over his face as he turned to look up at Mrs. Hollingsworth. "She's okay." His tone of voice was calm as he stood up from his chair and walked over to a glass-doored cabinet in the corner of the study. He opened the middle drawer and pulled out a small Walthur automatic, walked over to the chair again and placed his foot up on it, rolled up his right trouser leg, and fastened the gun snugly into an ankle holster over his black Christian Dior sock. He continued talking to Mrs. Hollingsworth as though he had merely tied his shoelaces and she listened without expression. Over the years she had grown familiar with Kevin's eccentricities.

"Guy sounds pretty much okay, don't you think?" he asked her.

"Sounds pretty much okay, Kevin," she replied, smiling, "Now what, Ocean City?"

"You got it."

"Want me to come along?" asked Mrs. Hollingsworth.

"No, I'll go." He paused, this time walking over to his bottom desk drawer and pulling out a leather shoulder holster that held a 9mm and began strapping it on. "Watch things for me?"

"You got it," she responded jokingly. "Kevin," she continued, "Why not just go straight to the hospital?"

"I want to meet these guys who found her." He kissed Mrs. Hollingsworth goodbye and said, "Go tell the others for me. Tell Megan I'll call from the hospital." He turned to leave through the side door.

"Bye, Kevin."

The sound of his silver Jaguar starting up alerted Megan to his departure before Mrs. Hollingsworth had entered the room to tell her he was gone.

"They found her?" Megan asked.

"They found her," Mrs. Hollingsworth responded as she walked into the room. "She's all right and they're taking her to the hospital."

"Thank God," said Megan, as she again stood by the big, bay window, watching the Jaguar pull away, saying another prayer for Kevin.

Kevin always drove fast. It made no difference if he was in his '66 Corvair or his '84 Jaguar XLS. He loved it. He always had. As he turned the car out on to Highway 1, his right hand moved automatically to the mobile telephone near the gearshift. He called his friends who were patrolling in a helicopter over the Atlantic, former mercenaries he had worked with in Angola back in 1975 and served with in the Special Forces before that, Bill and Joe.

"Bill?"

"Major." Bill responded, paying no attention to standard radio-operating procedure. "We heard the call. We're about fifteen minutes away from them. Want us to take her?"

"No, just watch from a distance. Sounded like the Coast Guard was gonna let these guys take her on in to Ocean City. Just make sure they get in and then take off. I'll meet them there." Kevin paused. "Thanks guys." Kevin hung up the phone and knew he was about twenty minutes from Ocean City at ninety miles-per-hour.

If it had not been for the storm he would have brought his Harley Roadster. Of all his bikes he loved it the best. Now, as he raced along the highway, passing through Bethany on his way south, his mind was on his bike.

It began to rain, at first just a drizzle and then a steady rain. The car handled beautifully and when the four-point buck became visible through his windshield Kevin knew he was going to hit it. The impact was sudden. Braking only a split-second before hitting the deer allowed him to bring the car to an abrupt halt without going into a spin.

He reached for the phone, not even bothering to get out of the car to inspect the damage. He had felt the steering column snap and knew he could not go any farther in the car.

"Bill?" he called.

"Major?" Bill answered.

"I've got a problem. Looks like a change of plans. Follow the boat in first, make sure it gets in, and then head north up Highway 1. You'll see me."

"What happened?"

"Car trouble." Kevin explained.

"You okay?"

"Yea," Kevin paused before continuing. "I'll be waiting right here for you. We'll have to go straight to the hospital from here. They'll have her in an ambulance before we get back down to the marina. All right?"

"Whatever you say, Major. See you in awhile." Bill turned to Joe. They both grinned at each other before Joe noticed the boat below.

"I see it," said Joe.

"We got her in view Major. See you shortly." Bill sounded relieved. Below was Toby's Bertram fighting its way towards the coast.

Kevin sat in the car on the side of the highway as the rain washed away the blood from the pavement. The carcass of the dead deer hung defiantly from the left front bumper of the Jaguar.

He turned on the car radio to a Dover station and heard the last part of a news report on the storm. Hurricane David was moving due north, directly towards Cape Hatteras, North Carolina. It was about twenty miles from the coast and there appeared to be some question as to whether or not it would touch land at the Cape or move on around it. If it turned to the east at all it would miss the coastal point and begin to move north, gathering strength on its way up along the coast. If that should happen, the hurricane warning would be extended all the way up to New York, possibly even to Massachusetts. Kevin turned off the radio and sat in silence.

V

Toby reluctantly left the care of his boat with Ben and Osborn. Mike tried to convince him that his presence at the hospital wasn't necessary but that didn't work. Now, as they stood in the crowded corridor near the Emergency Room admitting desk, he was thankful Toby had come along.

The hospital was frantic as word quickly spread that the mayor of Ocean City was about to order a full evacuation. The already overworked and underpaid staff of the hospital had switched into high gear as they began to prepare for extreme overcrowding, unknown crises, and the inevitable general panic. There was only one major hospital in Ocean City. But now, even with the storm some seven or eight hours away, the rain and winds had already provided them with an unusually high number of accident victims, none of them terribly serious, but still enough to create a crowded admissions area.

Toby maneuvered to the front of a line of people waiting to sign in and somehow convinced the nurse at the desk that his situation was far more urgent than that of the others. Virginia was immediately trans-ferred to a bed in one corner section of a large examin-ing room and a frail, portable, folding partition was set up between her and the other patients. She was sleep-ing soundly from the medication the paramedics had given her in the ambulance to stop her from trembling. When Toby walked away from the admissions desk and announced to Mike and half the room that she would soon have her own room, Mike was grateful for the big man's presence.

He assumed, of course, that Toby's unique gift at persuasion had been instrumental in securing the room. As Toby stood beaming with self-confidence in front of him, Mike began to look around the room at the other pa-tients. For the first time since arriving he actually began to smell the hospital smells and hear the sound of doctors being paged. It seemed as though everyone in the room was either talking about the storm or sitting there quietly thinking about it. A 19-inch television screen mounted up on the wall began to carry a special report on the progress of the hurricane.

He and Toby stood restlessly in the waiting room and stared up at the television, trying to hear what the reporter was saying over the din of voices in the room, when all at once it seemed the others stopped talking and also began to stare quietly at the screen. The voice of the reporter became audible at once.

The reporter was a young man with blond hair and was wearing a bright yellow rain slicker, the hood of which was being tossed around the back of his neck by the gusting wind. He declared he was broadcasting from a small town about thirty miles west of Cape Hatteras which was soon to receive the brunt of the storm as the eye roared up the coastline only ten miles off shore. He was emphasizing the potential danger and urging the viewers to follow the advice of the authorities without question, suggesting that to flirt with a storm so big was tantamount to lunacy. He concluded by saying that he and the rest of a special eyewitness news team would stay right where they were, for as long as they could, to provide the best possible coverage for Channel 4 viewers.

"Fuckin' pussy," Toby muttered quietly to Mike.

Mike looked at Toby, right into his bright gray eyes, and knew that Toby actually believed this reporter truly was a wimp. "Think your boat will be okay?" Mike asked with no show of great concern, even casually.

"She'll be fine." Toby smiled, confident. "You know you sure worry a whole lot for a shrink."

"Psychotherapist," Mike responded.

"That's what I said, 'shrink'." Toby grinned.

"You go ahead and get back to the boat. I'm going to wait here," Mike suggested.

"I suppose you're right," Toby said with some hesitation as he stared up at the reporter in the bright, yellow slicker. He reached into his hip pocket and pulled out a folded Orioles baseball cap and placed it on his head. "I suppose you're right."

As Toby looked over towards the examining room where Virginia lay, frightened even in her sleep he imagined, he motioned to Mike that he wanted to go over and see her one more time before leaving. He took his cap off and held it nervously in his hands as he walked into the examining room with Mike right behind him.

The folding partition was drawn back and it squeaked with age as a flurry of activity was taking place around Virginia's bed. Two white jacketed orderlies were raising the side railings of her bed and beginning to wheel her in the same general direction from which Mike and Toby were approaching.

Kevin stood over her right side, holding her hand, walking in pace with the orderlies. As they passed close, Kevin looked up for a minute, then back down to Virginia as he let go of her hand. The orderlies kept moving and Kevin stopped. He slowly approached Mike with his hand outstretched.

"You must be the guys who found her." His gaze was intense and startled Mike.

"Mike Chandler," Mike said, shaking Kevin's hand, "and this is Toby Tarr."

Toby grabbed for Kevin's hand as soon as it fell from Mike's. "You're a very lucky guy Mr. Kepler."

"Yea," Kevin replied, almost impassively, "I know." Something in the tone of his voice indicated that he didn't feel particularly lucky. "I want to thank both of you. She's going to be fine, according to the doctor. She's going up to her room now. Might need some oxygen or something later. She's always had a minor respiratory thing." Kevin was rambling nervously.

Mike retorted, "She's a trooper. She'll be okay."

Where they had stopped to talk was an awkward place to stand and chat, with all of the activity around them. Aware of this, Kevin suggested, "Let me go up and check on her, then let's have a cup of coffee, all right?" He was moving away from them as he spoke. "I'll meet you in the cafeteria in ten minutes?"

Toby stood there, shifting the weight of his big frame back on to the balls of his feet and then to his toes, almost undetectably. He responded to Kevin, "I'm headin' back, gotta check the boat."

Kevin surprised both of them. "The boat's fine. I want to talk to you about that anyway. Just give me five minutes." He turned away and walked towards the elevators in the corridor.

"I'm still gonna go check the boat," Toby declared to Mike after Kevin had gone.

"You should, Toby. You should." Mike was still looking towards the corridor rather than at Toby.

"Wonder what he means about wanting to talk about the boat?" Toby pondered out loud.

"What?" Mike looked towards him, "Oh, about the boat? I don't know what he meant. Sounded like he'd taken care of it or something?"

Toby grew more concerned. "Yea. It did sound like that, didn't it." Toby put his arm on Mike's shoulder. "You gonna be okay down here without me?"

"Yea, fine," Mike assured him. "You just go. I'll be okay."

Toby walked away from Mike towards the front desk. Mike stood in the examining room for a moment before following him. It occurred to him that Toby might have trouble getting a taxi in such weather. Just as he turned the corner he heard Toby raising his voice with the admissions nurse, apparently having just been told the same thing. Mike walked over to Toby and tried to defuse the situation as gracefully as possible.

"Let's get some coffee, Toby," Mike offered.

Toby's agitated expression gave way to one of helplessness as he responded. "You go on to the cafeteria." He paused. "I wonder how much one of these ambulance drivers would charge me for a ride back."

"They're probably needed more here, Toby. Come on." Mike gestured for Toby to follow.

Toby stood there, looking perplexed, even sad, for a moment. Then he said, "You go on. I'll be there in a minute."

Mike smiled, presuming acquiescence, and walked away towards the coffee shop. Toby walked out towards the exit and saw the dark sky and the rain through the glass double doors on his way out.

Bill and Joe stood in the covered entranceway to the emergency room, both wearing greenish colored parkas and chatting with each other. Bill, his six feet two frame, thin yet taut, was taunting Joe, "You're a regular fucking Rambo, aren't you?"

Joe was discussing his latest fight. He had just told Bill how he had "kicked two guys' butts at the same time" last week when they tried to mess with him at a local tavern. Joe was always getting into fights. His frame was indeed about the size of Stallone's, although Joe was older and flabbier, and he had loved to fight his whole life. Bill, on the other hand, was a thinker, and a quick talker. The combination had proven to be a good one over the years and they constantly poked fun at each other's limitations. Toby marched purposefully into the same covered entranceway and almost walked directly into Joe. "Sorry," Toby muttered, staring at the rain.

Joe looked first at Toby, then at Bill, and then gestured with his arm towards the ocean. Bill nodded to Joe as he moved towards Toby and said, "Need a lift?"

Toby was stunned. He stared at the two of them before responding, "How'd you know?"

"Never mind that, Cap," Bill continued, "you're probably real concerned about that cruiser, right. I sure would be. Best place for that boat right now would be about as far away from this storm as you could get it, right?"

Toby stood listening, stupefied yet curious. "Right."

"Your guardian angel must be lookin' out for you." Bill extended his hand. "I'm Bill Rogers and this here is

Joe Blount, sometimes known as Rambo. We work for Major Kepler."

Joe slugged Bill good naturedly in the side before he extended his own hand to shake Toby's. "Joe Blount, please to meet you, sir."

Toby inquired hopefully, "You guys got a car?"

Joe smiled at Bill who was still grimacing from the shot in the ribs he had taken.

"Well, we do have an excellent means of transportation, if that's what you mean," said Joe, grinning, referring to the helicopter parked on the edge of the parking lot.

"Well," said Toby, unknowingly, "let's hit the road."

VI

Mike sat at the counter in the coffee shop staring into his second cup of coffee. Over fifteen minutes had passed and Kevin had not arrived. A few minutes earlier he had gone out to check on Toby but couldn't find him. He asked a few people if they had seen him, but no one had. As he stared into his cup he began to think about Virginia and crazy feelings surrounded his thoughts. As much as he fought it, he felt a growing infatuation for the girl. But then he thought about Marcia, the woman he shared his life with in Annapolis, perhaps the future Mrs. Chandler, what about her? His feelings for Marcia were kind of like the feelings one might have when an old friend comes to mind. Warm, pleasant, even exciting, but hardly romantic. He closed his eyes and pictured Virginia's beautiful face against the stark white pillow.

Her dark red hair shining in the bright fluorescent lighting of the examining room, glowing in the subdued lighting of the cabin on the boat, glistening in the sporadic, dim, interior lighting of the ambulance. He felt totally responsible for her as though she represented everything he held precious in life, and it was all happening very quickly.

He stood up and placed a dollar on the counter, his eyes searching through the small glass windows in the metal swinging doors that led to the kitchen for a sign of the waitress. He was startled by the sound of Kevin's voice behind him. "Let's get a booth. Sorry I'm a little late." Kevin's voice was full of calm. Kevin began to talk as soon as they sat down, almost as though he had been asked some highly personal question and for the first time in his life was going to give the real answer. All Mike had asked was, "How is she doing?"

"She's sleeping." He paused before continuing. "You know I remember when I was about, oh, thirty-one or thirty-two, Virginia was still a baby. Well, a toddler. She hurt her head one night. Running around the house like crazy. Ran right into the open refrigerator door. I didn't know what to do. Her mother was out somewhere. There was Virginia, all sprawled out on the linoleum floor, blood pouring out of a cut on her forehead. I rushed over to the sink and got a washcloth, soaked it good, and brought it over to her and held it tightly against the wound. She screamed so loud. Her eyes were flooded with tears, like little pools of water completely covering her eyes, you know, overflowing out around the edges. And she screamed and screamed. We had a wall phone in the kitchen right above where she was and I reached up to grab it and dialed 911." He paused as the waitress set the hot tea he had ordered in front of him and mumbled a thank you to her.

"Anyway, I couldn't hear the operator, her crying was so loud. So I just picked her up and walked over to the drainboard to a dish where we kept all the car keys, got the keys to an old '56 Buick Special we had, it had vinyl seats, and walked out the door with my screaming little girl. It was still early evening and I remember worrying about the neighbors hearing our baby screaming, even though it was good hundred yards to the neighbor's house. Somehow, I got her into the car and rested her head on my lap, still holding the washcloth across her forehead, and drove about fifteen miles to the hospital. She took thirteen stitches in her head." Kevin paused again, gazing out the glass picture window of the coffee shop into the atrium of the hospital on the other side. "I remember it all so clearly."

Mike realized Kevin expected him to reply. "Same hospital?" he offered quickly.

"No, no." Kevin looked out towards the atrium. "Not this place. No, it was a place in upstate New York." He was silent for a minute, as though thinking about something very important.

"Is that where you're from?" Mike asked. "Upstate New York?"

"Well, on the Hudson, near Croton, not really upstate I guess," Kevin said this as though he were still thinking of something else, preoccupied with some other thought.

Mike stared at him, wondering what it might be. Suddenly, Kevin continued, "I was still commuting back and forth a lot. Her mother and I were very, very happy then." He took a sip of his tea. He looked as though he'd found his thought and was focusing on it. "She was beautiful."

"Virginia's mom?" Mike asked.

He looked down at his cup. "She died in a plane crash ten years ago." He was monotone. Then his tone of voice picked up as he added, "Now I'm married to a lady named Megan, a real neat lady." He seemed okay again before adding, "You saved my daughter's life. I owe you my own."

Mike grinned, replying, "Nonsense. It was nothing. You owe me nothing."

The grateful expression on Kevin's face became very serious. "Oh. I do. And I will make it up to you one way or another."

To change the subject, Mike asked, "So what were you doing up in Croton?"

"I was a cotton trader," Kevin answered.

"A what?" Mike asked.

"A cotton trader. You know, cotton futures," Kevin explained. "I worked on the trading floor of the New York Cotton Exchange."

"How did you get into that?" Mike asked.

"Oh, by accident, I guess. I knew this guy, a friend of my father. He was a big shot down there on the floor and one day he asked me if I would be interested." Kevin had completely regained his composure. "That was so long ago."

"You still trade cotton?" Mike was curious.

"Not from the floor," Kevin said. "I'm more interested now in other things."

"Like what?" Mike asked.

"International trade," Kevin responded, grinning.

"What do you mean?" Mike asked.

"Oh, armaments mostly." Kevin appeared to be uncomfortable. He took his jacket off as though he had been too warm, his shoulder holster visible to everyone now.

Mike was eager to learn more and tried to ignore the gun. "How did you get into that?"

"Well," Kevin began, "I'm not sure if I ever really got out of it. You see, I went to work for an arms manufacturer right after the fall of Saigon and actually stayed over there for a while. Made a lot of good contacts." Kevin felt comfortable in telling Mike about himself, but he was sure to only tell him as much as he wanted him to know. "I stayed in touch with them. When I sold my seat on the exchange I set up my own business."

Mike was surprised. "Arms sales?"

"Yea, you know. Selling guns and ammunition to countries for their military," Kevin explained.

"Which countries?" Mike felt like he might be prying a little too much.

"Whoever wanted to buy them," Kevin answered. "Back then it was mostly Mid-Eastern countries."

"Did you get to see Virginia much?" Mike asked. "Or were you out of the country a lot."

"I was home a lot of the time." Kevin refilled his teacup from the small teapot in front of him. "Probably more than when I was trading on the floor. Those hours were really brutal."

"You were living in Croton?" Mike asked. "And commuting to the city."

"Yea, but it didn't last too long. I bought a ranch in Virginia when I got out of futures."

"A horse ranch?" Mike guessed correctly.

"Yea, she's loved to ride horses ever since she was little." Kevin's face was showing the pride he felt for his daughter.

"A lucky girl," Mike offered.

"Everything was really very wonderful until her Mom died." Kevin's face grew somber again.

"When Virginia was about seven?" Mike asked, having done the math.

"Yea. Almost eight, actually. It was almost time for her birthday. I remember how excited she was and how hard it was to tell her that her Mom was gone."

The waitress came over to check and see if they needed anything. Mike asked for a glass of water and Kevin shook his head no.

Kevin addressed Mike, "So what do you do?"

"I'm a psychologist. I have a small practice in Annapolis," Mike responded.

Kevin looked surprised, as if he had expected something else. "Really," he remarked. He stirred his tea a minute without saying anything. Then, looking up at Mike he said, "We went through quite a few of you guys for awhile, you know." Mike was slightly offended and Kevin offered, "I didn't mean it like that."

"That's all right. I imagine Virginia was a mess over the loss of her mother." Mike's voice had taken on a tone he used with his patients.

"As a matter of fact, she handled it very well. I meant her step-mom, Megan. She's had a real hard time with life. Nothing specific. Mostly just bad nerves. We went through a period where I think she went through about five therapists. Then she got better."

"Through therapy?" Mike supposed.

"No." Kevin paused. "Jesus. She really got into it, and it worked. She's a different person, now. Not a born-again evangelical, just, well, she seems at peace with herself."

"Really?" Mike was trying to be polite and show some enthusiasm, although he had very little for this subject. He had lost too many patients to Jesus. It was always when he was just about to work out their problems, too. "I'm happy for you, really, I am." He sounded sincere.

"But if she ever needs any help again I'll certainly think of you," Kevin offered. He then mentioned the storm for the first time. "Ever been through a big hurricane?" He sounded as if he had personally been through several.

"No, I haven't. I've managed to stay out of their way." Mike sounded relieved.

"This David is a serious storm," Kevin said.

"The guy on the news said they still didn't know which way it was going. You think it could come through here?" Mike asked.

"Sure. It could. We won't know for awhile. But I wouldn't worry about it. We'll have enough advance warning to get out of the way."

"I guess you're right. Are you going to leave Virginia here?" Mike inquired.

"For awhile at least. If it looks bad with the storm I'll move her over to Salisbury, or Hopkins."

"How will you do that? Won't the roads be too crowded?"

"Fly her over. I figure in another hour or so we'll know more about David. I've got a chopper here and an ace pilot if we need it. As soon as they get back from Ocean City, that is."

Mike was stunned. "A chopper?"

"Yea."

"But what about the wind, won't it—" Mike asked.

"It'll be a rough ride but no big deal. As long as we get out of here in time. You see, a hurricane's wind is only too strong for a helicopter if you get too close." Kevin grinned. "We simply better not get too close, that's all." He then stood up and put on his jacket. "Want to go check on our girl?"

As they stood in the corridor waiting for the elevator, it became more obvious to them that the level of activity in the hospital was escalating. An old black man with silver hair and sideburns and a very dark face lay on one of the rolling beds in the hallway, abandoned there. He spoke to Mike and Kevin, and as he spoke his red tongue darted in and out of his mouth and seemed to make his dark skin look even darker. His nose was flat and pressed up against his face, his nostrils flaring wildly as he spoke.

"This gonna be a bad one, a reeeel bad one! I ain't neva seen it like this before." He was excited as he spoke. Mike and Kevin smiled at him, then at each other.

Kevin asked him, "They just leave you out here in the middle of the hall?" He spread his arms out to indicate the area.

"Yea they sure did. And I be all worried about my family and everything." He was very concerned, as if he believed his family was in great danger.

"Where is your family?" Mike asked.

"In Pittsburgh, worried sick about me." And the old man began to laugh and laugh, thoroughly delighted with himself.

Kevin smiled at the old man as the elevator door opened and an approaching orderly moved the old man on to the elevator. Kevin and Mike followed him in as the doors closed silently. It was quiet again until the old man got off on the second floor.

"She's on the third floor," Kevin said.

"Old guy seems happy," said Mike.

"Yea, a little wacko, too," Kevin said softly, staring at the illuminated numbers above the door as they changed slowly from 2 to 3. Darkness swallowed up the elevator compartment as it came to an abrupt halt before the doors opened.

"Oh shit," whispered Mike.

"It's okay, relax," said Kevin without concern. "Probably just testing the back up generator." After a few seconds the power came back on and the doors opened noiselessly.

"Jesus Christ!" exclaimed Mike.

"They've got to make sure the automatic switchover is working like it should. They'll probably be hit with a major power outage later." Kevin sounded comforting to Mike, as though there was no cause for concern.

Mike followed Kevin to a room down the hall, his heart beating rapidly as they approached the door. Kevin knocked once and entered. They found Virginia sleeping peacefully, as far away from the reality around her as one could be, and she looked even more beautiful than ever. They stood watching over her, not saying anything for a minute or two, grateful she was going to be okay.

VII

Flying at about 3000 feet, Joe piloted the helicopter almost effortlessly through the dark sky over Eastern Maryland. Toby and Bill were getting along extremely well, talking and joking around about how many "pussys" there were down below that were getting all worked up about the storm for no good reason. Bill was asking Toby about his boat when the first strong gust of wind slammed into the chopper and knocked them over into a sideways position for a moment before Joe was able to regain control.

"Hey, Rambo. What the fuck?" shouted Bill. His voice showed a strain of concern even though he tried to cover it up.

"We're okay," Joe explained, and just then another blast of wind slammed into them. As Joe recovered from this second disruption, he turned to look at Bill. Without saying anything the expression on his face begged Bill to let him go for it.

Bill though for a minute. Toby stared at Bill's face and it was obvious that Bill was very quickly weighing all of the reasons why they should or should not go on. The thought of uttering "pussy" did not occur to Toby. The impact had been so sudden and forceful that even he was alarmed, adrenaline pumping through his veins as he kept silent. Bill was still thinking about their options when a third and even more violent blast of wind hit them.

The chopper turned over, nearly 90 degrees, as Joe struggled to regain control. Bill was shouting, "TAKE HER BACK, JOE. TURN IT AROUND. FUCK THIS!"

Joe regained control and was able to turn the helicopter around, at the same time descending to an altitude of about 1500 feet. The gusting wind had less effect on them at this level and within minutes they were flying smoothly again, heading west, back towards the hospital and away from the Ocean City coastline, Ben and Osborn, and Toby's boat.

After a few minutes passed in silence, Toby addressed Bill, "So what exactly did Kepler mean when he said he had taken care of the boat?"

"He meant that you, me, and Joe would go back and try to make her as safe as possible," Bill answered.

"Oh," Toby said despondently, "that's what I figured." He then added, "I hope those two bastards Ben and Osborn stay sober long enough to take her into a marina and tie her up." For a moment Bill thought Toby was going to insist they go back for the boat, but he didn't make a sound.

"Heh, big guy. It's just a boat. It'll be fine. Might get bounced around a bit but it'll be fine. I'd be more concerned about your two pals getting out of the boat and getting to a safe place than I would be about the boat," Bill offered. Then he turned to Joe. "Get the guard on the radio, Joe." Then back to Toby. "We'll ask 'em to watch over it if they can. If they won't listen to us we'll have the Major call 'em. They'll listen to him."

Toby did not respond. Instead he sat motionless, staring out the window towards the ocean, as if he were mentally picturing the total destruction of his boat and a big part of himself as it happened.

CHAPTER 2

Megan stood staring out the big picture window of the house at Fenwick Island, watching the heaving motion of the sea as the weather grew worse. While wringing her hands together nervously and praying to her savior for calm, the telephone rang.

"Hello?" She answered it.

"Hi hon." It was Kevin. "Listen, Virginia seems to be fine. I'm trying to start working on a move, with the storm and all, and I..." he paused, "I think you and Jimmy and your father ought to get out of there." He sounded much more concerned than he had the first time he had called, before Bill, Joe and Toby had gotten back to the hospital after failing to reach the boat. He was unsettled from the report Bill had given him about the wind; he hadn't expected the wind to be that strong so soon. The storm was still over one hundred miles away. "So," he continued, "pack an overnight bag and the three of you get out of there. Stay off the Coastal Highway. Take DuPont up to the 404 and then take that to the 50. Take that over to your sister's place in Baltimore. It's almost noon, you should be there by about three-thirty or four."

Megan stood there, patiently listening to his instructions. She wondered why, but only for a moment, he could not come get them. Then she asked, "What are you going to do with Virginia, Kevin?"

"And tell the Hollingsworths they should come with you. Tell them I said so." He did not answer her question.

"And Virginia, and you? Where will you be?" she asked again.

"We'll be here a little while longer, then on to Hopkins, probably," referring to Johns Hopkins Hospital in Baltimore.

Megan knew the answer to this next question as she asked it, "And you two are flying over, right?"

"Yea, that's right," Kevin answered. "Listen, I gotta go. Call me later from your sister's house."

"I will," she replied.

"Yea. Call me from there. Now, get moving. I want you all out of there by one o'clock."

"We will be," she told him, adding, "I love you."

"Love you too. See you soon," said Kevin.

"Bye." She hung up and immediately began to pray again, asking Jesus to help her get through this. When she was finished, she called for Jimmy. He came in from the next room and she explained to him what they were doing.

"Cool!" Jimmy exclaimed. "Uncle Kevin flying up there? Man, I wish I was with him."

"I know how excited you are, Jimmy." Megan put her arm around her nephew and walked with him towards the adjoining room, where her father and Mr. and Mrs. Hollingsworth were still watching television. "I know how excited you are." She repeated herself as they entered the room. "Storm must be getting pretty bad?" she began.

"They just had a broadcast. You missed it," her father announced loudly. "Damn things coming our way!" His spectacles bounced up and down on his nose in his excitement as he looked up at his daughter.

"Kevin wants us all to go to Baltimore." She looked over at Mr. and Mrs. Hollingsworth and added, "All of us."

"Right now?" Mrs. Hollingsworth asked.

"Right now," Megan said. "Jimmy, go pack your things, quickly. Dad, I'll help you." Jimmy bounded up the stairs, with Grandpop close behind mumbling something about 1934 no one could make out. Megan turned again to the Hollingsworths. "He said to tell you—" she started.

"I know, I know. He wants us to come too. Come on Donald, let's go pack." Mrs. Hollingsworth addressed her husband, a small quiet man in his mid-sixties who seemed as though he lived his life simply to do as he was told.

"Okay," he responded without question, "let's go." As he stood up he looked like a genuinely happy man.

"Megan," said Mrs. Hollingsworth as she led her husband to the front door, "we'll be back in a jiffy."

Megan stood in the doorway for a moment after they walked out, both of them huddled under an old pink umbrella, watching them cross the front lawn in the rain. She watched them admiringly, hoping one day she and Kevin would also be so close and so happy.

Kevin was standing at the admissions desk when he hung up the phone. He leaned over to sign some papers the nurse had prepared for him to release his daughter. This nurse did not know Kevin, and she thought he was crazy to be checking his daughter out under the circumstances. She felt extremely anxious as she watched him sign the papers that would allow him to take Virginia out of the warm, safe, confines of the hospital and whisk her off in a helicopter, of all things, and in this storm. And with those three other odd looking characters standing over in the lobby! Toby, Bill, and Joe did look somewhat out of place as they stood waiting for Kevin, none of them particularly knowing what would happen next.

Upstairs in Virginia's hospital room, Mike sat in a chair he had pulled up next to her bed. He was feeling her forehead to make sure she was no longer running a fever when she opened her eyes.

"Where's Dad?" she asked.

"He's downstairs, checking you out of here," Mike explained.

"I'm leaving? How long have I been here? It seems like—" Virginia sounded confused.

"Relax. Only been here a couple of hours. Feel any better?" he asked.

"I—" she paused.

"Hurricane David has become much bigger than people thought he would. Your Dad's just playing it safe," Mike explained.

"What's going on? Is it coming this way?" she asked.

"Well, it's coming up along the coast at a pretty good pace," he explained.

"I know he must be really upset," she said.

"It's a big storm. Your Dad's just—" Mike started to explain.

"I know. That's just Dad." She smiled and her face lit up as she responded, "He's a nut."

Mike felt awkward for the first time in the conversation as he said, "I don't think the helicopter has enough room for all of us."

"Joe's chopper?" she asked, "*Ma Bell*?" As the ten year old Bell helicopter had been christened by Joe.

"Yea. I guess," Mike answered.

"Who's all of us?" she asked curiously.

Mike felt his face start to flush in embarrassment as he continued, trying not to let himself be too obvious. "Well, me and Toby…" he began, his face now bright red, "me and Toby were just sort of…."

"You and Toby what?" she smiled mischievously.

"Nothing. We were just thinking about coming along, that's all," Mike tried to explain.

"But why? What for?" She was grinning, still teasing him.

Mike looked into her eyes and felt some of the redness leave his face. He did not know what he was going to say, or if he was going to say anything at all. She looked back at him and he felt a certain rhythm of feelings, all falling into place; he almost felt euphoric for a moment. The longer he stared into her dark brown eyes, the more he felt it, until he was sure she must be feeling it too. And when she didn't say anything, and only stared back at him, smiling, he felt that at the least there was now some understanding between them.

"Why would you want to be coming with us anyway?" she asked again, this time the smile on her face giving way to an expression of seriousness.

He did not, rather, he could not answer her immediately.

"Mike?" she asked, "Are you all right?"

After a long moment of silence, he was able to respond, "Yea, I'm all right." He was looking down at the floor rather than into her eyes. He had begun to blush again in his embarrassment.

"What's wrong?" She reached out and felt his forehead this time. "You sure you're okay? Maybe the cold and the wet got to you too?" Her voice was full of concern. She was obviously disturbed by the sporadic flushing of his face and his peculiar behavior. She had no idea what he was experiencing and only thought he was probably coming down with a cold.

"No. I'm okay. Really." He felt nauseous in the pit of his stomach and mentally disoriented. "I guess I might be getting a bit of a chill." He stood up and put the chair back up against the wall. "Listen," he continued, "I'd like to check on you. You know, make sure you come through this thing okay? Know what I mean?" He even surprised himself with the degree of calm he displayed in asking to see her again.

"Fine." Her eyes sparkled. "Just give me a call?" It did sound like she wanted to see him again, or so he thought.

"1 will. But how do I do that? I mean, I don't even know where you live. I don't even have your number." He knew he sounded too excited, but he couldn't contain it.

"I'll be at Dad's, or I'll be at—" she said as her face grew ashen and a sudden sadness breached her countenance. She began to cry, remembering that Nathan was gone forever. Grief overwhelmed her and she cried for the first time since the incident. And as Mike stood there next to her, holding her hand and trying to comfort her, he thought to himself how healthy all this was for her, letting go of her grief. He even began to think that he was glad it had all happened, until he too was struck with the tragedy of the situation. It was at this moment that a single knock was heard on the door and Kevin entered with Bill, Toby, and Joe walking in behind him, Joe noisily pushing in a stretcher on wheels.

"Heh, what's this?" Bill exclaimed as he smiled at Virginia and immediately walked over to her, taking her hand out of Mike's hand and holding it in his own. "No tears. It's wet enough already out there." Bill looked over at Mike who simply stared dumbly back at him. "Who's this?" he asked Virginia while still staring at Mike.

Kevin answered as he approached the bed, "This is Mike Chandler, Bill. He and Toby saved her life out there. Now let's get the show on the road. Joe, you get over there." He motioned to the other side of the bed. Two orderlies were standing helplessly in the doorway. Having offered to help them move her and having been rebuked by Kevin, they were now watching Bill, Joe, and Kevin move Virginia on to the smaller, more portable, rolling bed.

Once she was settled in the new bed, with Bill and Joe on either end of it to help move her out of the room, she looked up at Toby and Mike. She had stopped crying and wanted to thank them for everything. As she turned to say goodbye she gave a sheepish grin and said, "Thank you guys," just as Bill and Joe began to wheel her out of the room.

Kevin walked over to them and shook hands, thanking them both again, before he too left the room. Mike and Toby stood staring at each other. Toby broke the silence when he said to Mike, "Let's get out of here."

"How's the boat, Toby?" Mike asked, not yet having had the opportunity to hear about the ill-fated rescue attempt.

"I don't know," said Toby, as they both walked out into the hall. "But I sure as hell would like to find out."

As Mike and Toby walked out of the room, Mike turned to look down the hall just in time to see the elevator door close behind Virginia. It suddenly occurred to Mike that he still did not have her number. With a look of mild alarm, he rushed down the hall to the elevator without saying a word. Toby stood outside the room door, quietly observing Mike's strange behavior.

"I'm going down to meet them," Mike shouted back to Toby as he walked through the stairway door beneath an illuminated exit sign.

Toby walked down the corridor to the elevators and decided to press the button and wait for a lift. In his mind, he began to wonder about Mike, and a suspicion of what was actually taking place suddenly hit him. "Now isn't that romantic?" he said to himself as he got onto the elevator, shaking his head in dismay.

Mike rushed down the steps two at a time. When he reached the first floor and threw open the door to the lobby level, he realized he was not really sure of the helicopter's location. What if it was on the roof? They would be boarding it at the same time he stood there thinking about it. He looked around and saw no sign of them. He turned and raced back up the stairs, passing the second floor door, then on to the third and the fourth, where the steps came to an end and he furiously pushed open the rooftop door.

The gray sky looked slightly green off to the southeast, the direction he was immediately facing as the door swung open. The sound of the helicopter was not loud enough. He ran out on to the roof into the drizzle and saw no sign of it. He walked quickly over to the edge and looked down over a small retaining wall which ran around the side of the pebbled surface. The helicopter was there, five floors down, and they were loading her stretcher on to it. Then they followed her inside. The noise of the blades grew louder as the helicopter lifted off the ground. Mike watched as it gracefully rose up and moved off to the left, over a small open area of the hospital grounds, and then it was higher than he was and racing away towards the north.

As his eyes moved slowly back down to the grounds below he saw Toby, standing in the rain, wearing his Orioles baseball cap. Mike's heartbeat quickened as he realized Toby might have gotten the number. He turned and walked quickly back into the stairway landing and closed the door behind him. He descended the steps in an almost leisurely manner, whistling the melody of a Springsteen song he didn't know the name of. Once down on the main level, he walked out through the side entrance to where Toby still stood outside in the rain. It was a warm rain, and not very heavy. Toby was lost in thought as Mike approached him. "Well?" Mike asked, "Did you get the number?"

Toby reached in his pocket and pulled out a dog-eared, yellowish business card with a small green helicopter in the upper left-hand corner and BOARDWALK COPTER RIDES printed across the face of it in bold type. In the lower right-hand corner was a name, an address, and phone number for Joe Blount. He handed it to Mike.

"Thanks Toby," Mike said as he stared at the card and then looked back up at the big man across from him, "I owe you. Heh! You're getting soaked!" Toby's cap was starting to feel the effects of the rain as water poured off the visor.

"Yea, guess it is starting to come down pretty good." They began to walk back into the hospital. "They shouldn't have no problems," Toby said, once back inside.

"What do you mean?" Mike was startled.

"They'll be just fine. Brunt of it's to our south, anyway." Toby was remembering his own brief copter ride!

"Yea," Mike began, "these guys seem to know their stuff pretty well." He was trying to sound confident.

Toby laughed and changed the subject, "Some fishing trip, huh?"

"I been meaning to talk to you about that," Mike replied, smiling.

"You know," Toby began, "it's really difficult to believe her boat just fell apart out there. I wonder what really happened." Toby's tone of voice now sounded curious, almost suspicious.

"What do you mean?" Mike responded, innocently.

"Well, I don't know for sure. It just seems like..." Toby stopped.

"Seems like what?" Mike prompted him anxiously.

"It almost seems like another boat just smashed right into 'em," Toby suggested, not meaning to sound preposterous at all.

Mike was surprised, "Well," he paused, "what would have happened to the other boat?" He sounded slightly defensive.

"Depends on what size it was," Toby explained. "Boat big enough could've just kept on going."

"Without even knowing it?" Mike asked in disbelief.

"Could have happened that way," Toby answered, "or it could've been another small boat. Could've gone down with the other part of that cat, too."

Mike began to feel unsteady, even a little lightheaded. He said nothing else.

Toby said, "We gotta figure a way out of this place. Either that or we get a ride going north. I sure as shit don't plan on spending the rest of the day around here." He began walking away from Mike, saying, "Come on, follow me."

II

Kevin was watching Virginia's face as she lay resting on the stretcher. Joe and Bill were in the front of the helicopter and the ride was surprisingly smooth, given the weather outside. Kevin's eyes were focused intensely on her face, or so it seemed at first. Actually, it was more of a blank stare and his mind was racing with thoughts of his past.

He thought of the various deals, all of the people that had, conveniently, come out on the short end of the stick, as he was so fond of saying. Many times he had orchestrated the sale of a huge shipment of arms, coordinating the diverse elements of the transaction, and often times squeezing out other less aggressive dealers in the process. He first thought of Roberto Valdez.

Valdez was now living in Cuba, a sometimes house guest of Fidel, or so rumor had it, and his ties with anti-imperialistic forces in Central and South America were legendary. Never mind that Valdez himself had absolutely no taste for Socialism. In fact, he detested the whole concept. Yet, it had been so lucrative for him, so "good for his career," as Castro had so often reminded him, that he had settled for a public support of the people's cause and a private displeasure at the whole concept.

Kevin had first crossed Valdez's path in Cairo, back in 1969, when Valdez had been introduced to him as a possible courier for a package of photographs that were earmarked for a Special Forces Command Unit in Thailand. He had instantly struck Kevin as one not to be trusted. Kevin had brought down all the heat he could manage in an effort to crack him, and it had worked magnificently. He broke Valdez's cover and brought him very close to losing all credibility with his own side. It took him years to regain his momentum again, and when he last saw Kevin, he swore he would make him pay for it. He had specifically threatened the life of Kevin's family. Though now, in retrospect, Kevin felt sure this was none of his doing.

He then thought of the others, the ones he had jumped in front of, not so much maliciously as cleverly, the millions of dollars they had missed out on, the careers that would never be the same again, the professional and personal relationships that had been ruined, simply because he had been better at the game.

His mind was now clear as he watched his daughter, occasionally looking up at Bill and Joe, then maybe back towards the southeast, but mostly at her. Someone had almost taken her away from him. He did not know who or why, he simply knew the reality of it, and it hurt more than anything else they could have done to him.

He was sure of it this time; it was nothing like the quiet uncertainty that had haunted him for a year after losing his wife Liz. It had been a commercial airline flight, hundreds had lost their lives, and even the FAA had given a reasonable explanation for the cause of the crash. Even so, he still had the year of doubt, a year of intense self-examination and rejuvenation before he had finally cleared his mind of it. And now, this.

The thing that bothered him the most was that he had no control over it. With all of his wealth, power, and contacts, he was still no more than an easy target for some twisted mind, and as he gazed again towards the southeast he was aware of the deceptive tranquility looming in the eye of this storm.

It could have come from Libya too, and he thought of that one crazed French mercenary, Dubre, who had been a hero figure to a small band of Libyan insurgents Kevin had come up against in Chad in 1973. They had come across the border on foot and were attempting to interfere with a drop of arms he had arranged for Chad's national army. The guns and ammunition were needed desperately by the government troops on the northernmost fringes of Chad and Kevin had given his word to an important group of people in France that he would make delivery. The Libyan guerillas were using extremely unsophisticated ground to air rocket launchers, yet as simple as they were in design, Kevin knew that one good hit would bring down the cargo plane carrying his shipment. From a relatively safe vantage point, Kevin had given the order for two helicopter gunships he had kept in waiting some distance away from the drop site, an order to eliminate the small band of guerillas before they destroyed his cargo plane. Later, the foreign press had called it a massacre, after Libyan-controlled insurgents completely toppled the national government of Chad. And Dubre was reportedly heard to have issued a death sentence against whoever had been responsible for the slaughter of his men. Whether or not he had ever found out it was Kevin who issued the order was still unknown. However, Dubre was certainly a possibility.

Kevin's mind ran through a series of events, thinking through all of the possibilities, but none of these scenarios he worked out gave him any idea who it might be that was trying to hurt his family. And, through all of this, he never once thought of Cecil Clemenzi, and Cecil, knowing Kevin well, knew he would probably not think of him, at least not at first. It had been so very long ago, yet to Cecil it was still so fresh in his memory, so easy to recall, so very much more important than anything else at all.

III

The bright yellow incandescent bulbs of the WELCOME TO OCEAN CITY sign that shined as a beacon from the top of a huge billboard, just on the inside of the city limits, were shining a new message by noon: MAYOR ORDERS EVACUATION IMMEDIATELY. The miles of high rise condominiums that ran down the coast along the highway were all emptying traffic from their underground parking garages on to the damp, paved drives that fed into the main road. A town designed to handle heavy traffic patterns during the summer months was smoothly ushering thousands of people safely on their way north or west to safer ground. Patrol cars, blue lights flashing in the mist, drove through the older neighborhoods and broadcast the evacuation order, over and over again, from the loud speakers mounted on their rooftops. A steady drizzle and dark cloudy skies made the proceedings more difficult than the mayor had first thought likely, yet now that the traffic was moving, it seemed like the evacuation would probably be complete by about four o'clock, still some two or three hours before the storm was due to arrive.

The Quality Inn, adjacent to the Coast Guard station on Coastal Highway, had thinned out quickly. Occupancy had been low anyway, due to new construction going on that hindered access from Route 50. The manager and his wife were some of the last to leave at about one o'clock. They had left orders for all personnel to take off, which included Karl, the bartender, and most of them had eagerly departed. Karl, to the contrary, was still behind the bar, having a great time talking with a few remaining customers who had chosen to stick around.

He had been talking to these two guys since about eleven o'clock that morning, listening to an incredible story that changed very little with the more they had to drink. Ben and Osborn, seated at the end of the bar near the waitress station, were having a great time. The drinks were free, Karl was a great guy, and the TV behind the bar was a nice one, good picture and color. They were following the rampage of David as he made his way north. He had passed within ten miles of Cape Hatteras less than an hour ago and the shots of the damage were just now coming across.

A small tsunami, the first ever recorded along the Atlantic Coast, had swallowed up a small tavern on the eastern most section of the coastal point, where some locals had decided to wait out the storm over a few drinks. There was nothing much left of the tavern on the newsfilm. In fact, it was hard to even discern where the beach had been with the water line all the way up past the highway. A few pieces of timber were being tossed around in the surf. No bodies were visible and little else, other than the water, could be seen. The newscaster was saying that most of the sand dunes had apparently been flattened by an underground suction created by the wave.

Ben was telling Karl and Osborn how he had the whole thing visualized. "You see these guys, you know, having a drink like we are, just sitting there at this little old watering hole, up on the dunes next to the beach, taking it all in, you know." He paused, taking a drink from his glass, relishing the moment before continuing. "When all of a sudden this big motherfuckin' wave, they see it, it's still way out there a ways but they see it. And it starts to grow, gets bigger and bigger, and they're all laughin' and shit, you see. Anyway, by the time it gets to the shore it's what, maybe twenty or thirty feet high? Big, but not big enough to scare the poor fools. And they just keep on drinking, watching and drinking and laughing, a little less laughing maybe, but still laughing. Anyway, they're sitting up by the highway, dunes between them and the water, got it? Well, all of a sudden, the water behind the wave gets bigger than the wave, and at the same time the dunes start to sink, yea sink! The dunes get sucked down into the ground from the vacuum of this son of a bitch. And these guys, see, these guys…" Ben stopped, then with more concern he continued, "then these poor bastards all bite it, all at once, all at the same time, gone." Then he was silent.

Osborn and Karl looked on, stunned, and when they realized he was through they both said, "Jesus Christ," in unison before taking another drink from their glasses.

Osborn said, "Benjie you got one hell of an imagination." He sounded like he wanted to believe Ben had made up the whole story. It really didn't happen like that!

Karl looked up at the TV again to where a report from the Hurricane Center in Miami was just starting, saying, "Pipe down you two."

On the screen was Dr. Frank, the director of the center, talking about the latest guess on the path of the storm. It seems like Dr. Frank is always being asked the same questions, over and over again, and he never tires of them. He is equally as enthusiastic in answering a question the tenth time as he was the first, and for those who have seen this Dr. Frank, they know his enthusiasm well. The man is obsessed with storms, especially hurricanes, and he talks of them almost as though they were human, as if they had a spirit of some kind, and when he began to talk about David, his excitement was unbridled. He waved his hands around the blue, green, and purple weather map on the monitor screen next to where he was seated. He pointed with a subtle reverence to David's eye and said nothing for a moment. He then began to describe the power of a Category 5 storm, which is what David had become, with winds in excess of 160 mph.

He began to talk about the reconnaissance flights, the normal routine missions that were flown whenever a storm this big came along. He began to say how unusual it was this time. That because of the size of this hurricane, and the strength of the winds, some which had been recorded at 200 mph, the flights were being suspended. However, he assured the viewers that this was temporary. Once again, his hand passed over the purple eye and he became silent for a moment.

He began to talk again, this time about the change of direction they were noticing (just after the tsunami hit shore it seems) as David had turned to the northeast a few degrees, potentially freeing the Virginia, Maryland and Delaware coast from extensive damage. If it could grow in strength on its journey north it would create a catastrophic scenario for Long Island and all points north. Dr. Frank was sounding like the host of a late night television show for a second or two, before he was asked another question, about what would happen if the storm turned to the west again. How quickly could that change occur, what sort of problems, how much damage could it cause the cities and towns along the immediate coast, the Mid-Atlantic coast? A reporter inquired about Washington D.C. and asked if it was facing any potential danger.

Only one way that could happen, Dr. Frank eagerly explained, and that would be if the storm decided to move to the west over the next two hours or so, at which time it would be right at the mouth of the Chesapeake Bay, and yes, the bay was a large enough body of water for the storm to stay alive in and perhaps even grow. Once up into the bay, then up to Annapolis, well, Washington was only thirty miles away. But of course this would not happen. Never had before, although there was a Level 5 back in 1934 that had actually entered the bay. He was then asked another question. Again he was asked to identify the characteristics of a Category 5 storm, and his enthusiasm did not wane a bit as he began to explain it all over again.

"This guy's unfucking believable!" exclaimed Osborn.

"You said it," Ben agreed. "Heh Karl. Sounds like maybe we're okay?" He looked at his empty glass and then back up at Karl, grinning.

Karl poured new drinks for both of them, and then poured himself one. "1934 - Jeez. Can you imagine that? Storm moves into the bay, a God Damn hurricane no less?"

"Over fifty years ago," Osborn was getting tanked; it was as though he said this only to hear himself do the math. He gazed into his old-fashioned glass full of bourbon and ice cubes with an almost moronic expression on his face.

Karl and Ben were looking back up at the TV again when the Maryland Linen Company paneled truck pulled into the motel's covered entranceway. It stopped in front of the glass doors of the motel lobby and lounge and right across the parking lot from the Coast Guard Station.

Mike and Toby got out of the truck. In frustration, Toby had "borrowed" it from a parking level near a loading platform at the hospital. They had driven to the shore on back roads to avoid heavy traffic, roads only used by hunters according to Toby. They walked across the parking lot to the Coast Guard Station. Toby found his boat being well taken care of and he was told where he could find the rest of his crew.

CHAPTER 3

Cecil Clemenzi sat in his big, lime-green overstuffed chair in the great room of his Long Island home, sipping on a DietCoke (which he had finally switched over to after many years as a Tab drinker) and watched a special weather bulletin featuring the director of the National Weather Service, Dr. Frank, regarding the path of Hurricane David and the potential danger facing the East Coast from Virginia Beach all the way up to Massachusetts. Cecil was wearing a lot of gold jewelry for someone simply lounging around the house on a Sunday afternoon. A thick, gold chain hung around his neck and draped across his nearly hairless, olive-skinned chest. His fingers were adorned with too many rings, and on the wrist of his right arm he displayed a wide, ornately designed gold bracelet. His eyeglass frames were gold as well. His black, almost bluish, curly hair looked unkempt, as though he had washed and dried it yet not bothered to brush it. He drank his soda through a straw, a pinstriped straw with three different colors of stripe: red, blue, and green. He special-ordered these straws from the manufacturer in Toledo and had done so for years. They were the same straws his mother used to buy for him when he was a child, the only kind of straw he would use.

Cecil had just turned forty and was beginning to have a problem with his waistline. It had always been somewhat of a problem, even as a boy, but now it was getting out of hand. He took a steam bath every morning and evening, rode his exercise bike until he perspired profusely, yet he was beginning to move from overweight to fat and he hated it.

As he watched Dr. Frank's report on the storm, a storm that "could possibly" though "probably would not" cause major problems for New York, he stared at the multicolored straw and thought deeply, almost dreamily, about his childhood.

Cecil was born in Cleveland, Ohio and grew up in a quiet suburban neighborhood of tree-lined streets and ranch-style homes that changed very little over time, even after he moved away at eighteen. Built towards the end of World War II, it was a typical middle class neighborhood with a blend of Protestants, Catholics, a few Jews and no blacks.

His father was a shoe salesman, eventually a store manager, for the Buster Brown shoe store on Bartlett

Road, now known as Bartlett Highway, and Cecil's first memories as a chubby little Italian Catholic schoolboy were of the Saturday mornings he got to go to work with his father. He was placed in charge of the small, brightly painted, wooden merry-go-round in the rear of the store. As the younger children came in with their parents, it was Cecil's job to escort them back to the merry-go-round, leaving only one child at a time alone with his father to try on shoes. His father would always sell more shoes that way, having the mother's undivided attention (when she was not glancing back towards the rear of the store to check on the noisy kids) and even though he never really explained it to Cecil, that this was his motive, Cecil had always known that it was.

After school, as he walked home with his older sister, Rebecca, he was often the subject of ridicule from the non-Catholic kids on the block and even though he once got a bloody nose standing up to one of them, they really didn't bother him all that much. The warmth and security of his home was always enough to make him feel okay again, no matter how much his feelings had been hurt by the other kid's remarks. When his father had a swimming pool built in the back yard, Cecil loved how the other kids tried to make friends with him. He enjoyed, immensely, not letting them pull it off. He and Rebecca grew up to be great swimmers and had wonderful tans, in season, and very few friends.

Occasionally, Cecil would be invited to another boy's birthday party. He would surprise his mother by telling her that he really wanted to go. His mother would always buy the greatest presents. He would go to the party and take way too much time in finishing his hotdog or sandwich, watching as the other children grew restless, seeing the mothers become anxious as they waited for him to finish before serving the cake. He loved watching the faces of the other kids when the birthday boy opened the present from Cecil which was, of course, a much, much nicer gift than any of the others. Cecil liked going to birthday parties.

Mostly he liked to be alone in his room. As he grew into adolescence, and other kids were listening to Elvis, Cecil began to take a keen interest in opera. His mother had always played lots of it and he had never really cared for it. But at thirteen, one lazy summer afternoon while he was lying on his bed in his room, with the door cracked open just enough to let *La Traviata* through, he discovered masturbation.

From then on, all the way into his adult life, he would get aroused at the first sound of anything by Verdi. As for other classical composers, he tried nearly all of them and it just wasn't the same. For his fourteenth birthday he asked for and received his own record player. Now he would spend hours alone in his room, a great deal of the time pounding away at the wild musical wizardry and tremendous vocal outpourings of certain, special operatic scores. In the next room, his mother, often times sitting quietly in her rocker, multicolored yarn piled in front of her in a small heap on the forest-green carpet, would hum along with the music, very proud of her son.

Academically, Cecil was brilliant. His only weak area was history. He had a terrible time with the subject, from seventh grade all the way through high school.

Nevertheless, he still graduated with a 3.7 GPA. This, combined with a very high score on his ACT exam, assured him an academic scholarship at N.Y.U.

He left home at eighteen, leaving Cleveland and his loving mother, hard working father, and older sister behind. He traveled to New York by train, arriving at Penn Station late on a Saturday afternoon. When he got off the train and looked around at all the people, for a moment he felt as though he were still wearing his Catholic schoolboy's uniform and for a second he found himself feeling insecure, awkward, even a little frightened by his surroundings. At that moment he made a vow never to allow himself to be humiliated or intimidated again, not here in New York. Here he would be his own man.

His four years at NYU were rather uneventful. However, he did develop a passion for poker and discovered that he loved to gamble. Between his winnings from poker games and his success at picking the right football teams, he managed to accumulate approximately $5,000 over the four-year stay at NYU, which he carefully set aside for use after graduation. He majored in Business Administration and when he graduated, amid the turbulence of the 1968 protest movements, he was firmly established as a quiet, boring, uncaring, not going anywhere kind of a guy with his graduating class. His parents flew in from Cleveland for the ceremony and he had nobody to even introduce to them as a pal or fellow classmate, not that this was any great surprise to his parents.

His father suggested that he return to Cleveland and check out the job market back at home. Instead Cecil decided to stay in New York City, at least for the summer.

One Sunday morning, after a refreshing shower and a quick session with Verdi, Cecil was reading the employment section of the New York Times and saw a job that sounded interesting.

NEW YORK COTTON EXCHANGE
Seeking recent college grad. Entry level position.
Fast-paced work as order clerk on the trading floor.
(212) 241-8753

He knew what this job was because he had visited the New York Stock Exchange as part of an Economics assignment in his freshman year. He knew this job was not really at the stock exchange but he thought it would be very similar. He called the number in the advertisement early Monday morning and made an appointment to go down there and see somebody about it that afternoon at one o'clock. He got there a few minutes early and spent some time looking around the place. From a window on the second floor in the visitor's gallery he could see the trading floor below. The first thing that struck him was how much smaller this place was than the stock exchange. The floor was only about the size of a basketball court, though it was crowded with people and buzzing with activity. The floor was separated into two areas, divided by a long row of order desks and telephone stations. One side was given twice as much space as the other, and the trading pit was a circular affair about forty feet in diameter with four or five different levels, or grades, descending down towards the center. The smallest circular area in the center of the pit was about fifteen feet in diameter, and it was full of men in blue smocks with large plastic name-tags stuck to their chest. They were shouting at each other, gesticulating wildly, and throwing colored sheets of paper into the air. These pieces of paper were then picked up by younger looking guys, about Cecil's age, and they would run with them back over to the order desks and hand them to the order-clerk, who would then hand them another sheet of colored paper and they would rush back out into the pit again, where they would hand it to one of the traders standing along the edge of the pit. Sometimes they would push through the first two or three levels of traders, down towards the center of the pit, where they would hand it to someone down below.

This process seemed to repeat itself with no particular rhythm, varying in degrees of momentum, and on the wall along one side of the floor was a quote board that extended down the length of the wall. Red and green lights flashed on and then off next to a set of numbers that changed every few seconds, sometimes not moving for five or ten seconds and then quickly changing every one or two seconds. Loud clicking sounds from the relay switches behind the bold white numbered squares of the quote board were barely audible over the din of the shouting voices from the floor. On the other end of the room was the same sort of arrangement but covering a smaller area. Later Cecil discovered this was where the

Orange Juice contracts, a market with much less trading volume, were traded.

Cecil stood looking out over the trading floor from the gallery window at the maze below and knew, intuitively, that he would get the job. He could not explain it, he didn't even understand what was going on down there. He just knew he would get the job. And he did.

He started working there as a runner to get familiar with the different aspects of trading and also because they wanted him to start as a runner. Within a month he was assigned to his own station along the row of order desks overlooking the larger, more active Cotton pit. He took this as an indication they were pleased with him; most of the other clerks had started at the Orange Juice desk.

The amount of money he saw change hands each day, and how quickly it changed hands, excited him to such an extent that he had to consciously remind himself throughout the day, and even late at night as he tried to sleep, that he must be patient, that it had taken him four years to accumulate his money and it would take less than a minute to lose it if he made just one bad trade. He resolved this conflict by making a pact with himself: he would not put any of his money in the market until he learned everything in the world there was to learn about Cotton. This would take awhile, and it would give him the time he needed to learn more about futures trading. Still, every morning, at the sound of the opening bell he spent an anxious moment with temptation.

He worked diligently at his job and became well liked by most of the other clerks and runners. He moved from the small apartment near the campus he had occupied for the last four years, into a nicely furnished one bedroom apartment in Flushing. He commuted on the subway and saved all the money he could by eating at home as much as possible. Macaroni and cheese, frozen pizza, and TV dinners became his regular diet. He was making enough money to furnish his apartment nicely but he chose not to. Instead, he bought items at yard sales and flea markets on the weekends when he liked to take long walks through the neighborhoods of Flushing.

Once, he bought a color television set for fifty dollars. It was old and the dark brown plastic cabinet was all melted in around the picture tube as though it had been in a fire, yet it still worked. It was a 15-inch set and weighed about forty pounds, and he still remembered the twelve block walk home.

He was carrying the set on his left shoulder. The sun went behind the clouds for a minute and as he looked up he noticed a rain cloud directly above him. He quickened his pace, almost halfway home. As he turned left on to a side street that would shorten his journey by a block, he saw a gang of older teenage boys standing on the sidewalk in front of him. He thought briefly of turning around but decided against it. With a determined look on his face, he stared down at the pavement in front of him and walked towards them.

The boys were Puerto Rican, not really an official gang by the looks of them, and Cecil felt better when he realized they weren't black. One of them began to say something about "that ugly looking TV, man" as Cecil passed, still looking down at the sidewalk, and his mind raced back to his schooldays. None of the other Puerto Rican kids were saying anything about his television. One of them, he thought, did call him "Tubby," but he wasn't sure.

He was about ten feet past them when he felt the first drop of rain, then a few more, and suddenly it was raining. All at once it seemed the Puerto Ricans began to get louder, laughing at him, saying things he couldn't understand yet knew were not kind. He walked faster, and they followed him just as quickly. He reached the next corner and they were upon him, louder with their laughing and now using some words he did understand. One of them was making noises like a chicken and the others were close to him, as though they were going to try to push the TV off his shoulder.

He was so preoccupied in watching the menacing faces of the boys as they mocked him that he didn't even hear the car pull up to the stop sign at the corner. The look of surprise on the young hoodlum's faces caused him to turn and look behind him, and he now heard the engine of the yellow mustang and he saw the same thing they did.

A tall, thin, dark haired man in his thirties was holding a shiny 38 caliber revolver in both hands, resting his arm on the wet rooftop of the car, and his face was scowling at them through the rain, obviously ready to start shooting at the slightest provocation. The gang turned and fled, leaving Cecil standing there facing the armed stranger, whose threatening countenance suddenly changed into a warm, friendly face.

Cecil carefully lifted the television off his left shoulder and placed it on the wet sidewalk at his feet, without taking his eyes off the man or the gun. The man withdrew the gun and threw it back inside the car, turned to Cecil and said, "God damn spics!" His smile was the kind that caused others to smile.

Cecil began to thank him, clumsily, though earnestly, and before he had even finished the man gave him a friendly wave, got back in the car, and started to drive away. While Cecil was still stumbling over his own thoughts, the yellow mustang pulled away, leaving him alone at the intersection with still some distance between himself and home. He picked up the set and continued walking, safely arriving back at his apartment ten minutes later, quite confused over the whole incident. He thought of the man in the yellow car often, reminded of him mostly by the sight of the deformed, brown plastic cabinet of the television set that now occupied one corner of his bedroom. When he saw him again, several months later, stopped at a traffic light in the late August rush hour traffic, he felt compelled to run over and thank him.

The stranger rolled down the window, and as the light turned green, asked Cecil to get in the other side if he wanted to talk so he could cross the street. As he opened the door on the passenger side he was wondering why he had not been offered a ride the first time, when he could have really used it.

"Sorry about our last encounter," the stranger began, "would've given you a lift but I had to be somewhere real fast, know what I mean?" His New York accent was thick. "Heh. Name's Fratino. Louis Fratino. Yours?" He held his right hand out towards Cecil as he introduced himself. Once across the street, traffic came to a stand-still again.

"Cecil," he responded, studying this Louis Fratino carefully and quickly deciding a first name only would be adequate.

"Cecil, huh. Those punks try to rip off your TV?" Louis asked, then added, "fucking spics."

"I'm not quite sure what they were trying to do, though I'm glad you came along when you did," Cecil explained.

"Where you from, Cecil?" Louis Fratino asked, curious.

"Cleveland," Cecil answered.

"Oh yea. Cleveland. Couldn't place it, you know?" Louis said, referring to Cecil's own peculiar manner of speaking.

As they sat in the sweltering heat of the traffic, with the Mustang's air conditioning growling at top speed and blowing out a blast of only tepid air, Louis began to talk about horse racing. Cecil was transfixed, a subject he knew nothing about all of a sudden became the most interesting thing imaginable, and as he listened to Louis talk about the upcoming race that night he said nothing.

"It's more than a sure thing, know what I mean? I got it from more than reliable sources. Flashdance by three lengths in the opener, at least 20 to 1. Jesus, I can't wait!" Louis was so excited he was oblivious to the slow moving traffic. All Cecil could think of was how he could get to the bank in time to make a withdrawal. After all, he thought, if I put up $500 on this it could pay $10,000. It was meant to be. Why else would he have run into this guy again? If he lost, so what, only $500. But he wouldn't lose. He felt sure about it.

"How," Cecil began, "how do you, I mean, do you actually go to the race track to do this, I mean, to bet?"

Fratino looked at Cecil with a winning grin and answered, "You never bet the ponies before? You got any money?" He asked this as though Cecil might not have any money, the implication being that this was a game for only certain special people.

"Yes, I have money," Cecil said reluctantly. "Is there a minimum bet required?"

"Not really a minimum," Louis responded. "You just got to know what kind of money you're playing with. But this one, jeez, this one I'd bet the rent check on, know what I mean? " Louis winked and drove through another set of lights. They had traveled one block in five minutes. "You like to wager?" Louis asked.

"I've been know to wager here or there." Cecil paused before asking, "You think I might be able to go with you?" It was a Friday night and he had no other plans, and if he had he would have canceled them. "I'd like to try it."

Louis showed appreciative surprise. "Well, I'm taking my sister and her bozo boyfriend over tonight, you want to come along, that's fine. You gotta last name, Cecil?"

"Clemenzi," Cecil responded.

"Clemenzi," Fratino repeated, relishing the sound of a good Italian name. "Cecil Clemenzi."

Traffic opened up a bit and as they turned at the next block to get on the expressway, Louis was asking, "You wanna ride home?" He slowed down before committing himself to the entrance ramp as he inquired, "You live in Flushing, right?"

"That would be great." Cecil looked at his watch. It was 5:15. He still had until six to reach the bank. "Need to get to the bank." Cecil then, for the first time, smiled back at Louis.

Louis hit the accelerator and the car lunged forward on to the entrance ramp. "You got it, Clemenzi. Let's go."

That night Cecil won $10,000 on Flashdance by three lengths in the opener and broke even on the other races. More importantly, that was the night he met and fell madly in love with Louis Fratino's sister, Katherine. The best weekend of his life.

As he now sat in his easy chair, seventeen years later, and stared out at the surf on his small private beach, half listening to the director of the National Hurricane Center warn New York that a serious hurricane was on the way, and half thinking about that weekend, his telephone rang. It was Louis Fratino.

"Yes," Cecil answered his cordless phone, simultaneously turning down the volume on the television with the remote control.

"Terrible storm to be out sailing, wouldn't you say?" Louis began.

Cecil smiled, "I'd say. Sure wouldn't want my daughter out there with this kind of weather brewing."

Louis laughed. "Yea, or my niece. Hee, hee, hee." His laugh had a baritone sound.

"Clean job I take it, no hitches?" Cecil asked.

"Definitely had to be taken for a boating accident. They said they just cut right into the damn thing, broke it in two. Both her and her fiancé went down fast, water was rough."

Cecil smiled again, obviously pleased. "Louis," he began, "remember Flashdance?"

"How could I forget? You came out big. I give it all away in the next race. Story of my life."

"I remember it too. Just like it was yesterday." Cecil was sounding melancholic.

"That was a long time ago, Cecil, say, Kathy's up at Mom's place. You think this storm's worth worrying about?"

"No, not really. Not for us at least."

"Yea, guess you're right. Anyways, just wanted to let you know things went down just fine, get it?" Again he laughed.

"Thanks, Louis. See you later tonight at Mom's."

"Yea, see ya." Louis hung up.

As Cecil set the telephone down again and turned up the volume on the TV, he felt no remorse at all. He smiled at the thought of the pain Kepler would feel from this, losing his precious little girl in the ocean. Cecil had gotten him back and it felt good.

Later that day, as Cecil got ready to leave for dinner at his mother in law's house in Brooklyn, he felt uncomfortable about things. He couldn't quite pin it down, what was bothering him. He stood in the driveway, under the carport, resting his body against the open door of his white Cadillac Seville, and gazed out towards the ocean. He could see a small section of his patio and briefly thought about moving the white, wrought iron furniture to a safer place yet decided against it. His back yard emptied into a sandy stretch of dirty beach. Abandoned horseshoe crab shells dotted the sand. He was thinking about when he first bought the house ten years ago, before Kepler had destroyed his world.

He had been doing very well, trading the market on a fairly regular basis, and had even developed somewhat of a reputation around the exchange as a shrewd trader. He had built his small nest egg into a rather substantial sum over a five year period of time. He had quit his job as clerk after two and a half years at it and leased a trading membership from one of the old timers until he came up with the thirty grand necessary to buy his own. Then, on January 22, 1973, it happened. There had been a hard freeze in Florida the night before and most of the cotton traders were in the Orange Juice pit the following morning. Cecil had never traded the OJ market before and had presumed it operated the same as Cotton, which of course it did. The only difference was the appearance of two traders, both unknown to him, and both with very deep pockets. He remembered talking to Kevin Kepler (a fellow cotton trader that Cecil had grown to respect) about the two strangers. Kepler told him to "fade those guys in the spot" if he really wanted to learn something about commodity trading. "Fade those guys in the spot." Cecil still remembered the exact words. Kepler had been referring to the nearby contract for delivery, the January contract. There was no daily trading limit on the spot month and its price could move as high or as low as it chose to. The other futures months were contained by a daily trading limit above or below the previous day's settlement price. Cecil had never traded the spot month before and Kepler knew it.

The two strangers had been buying contracts since the opening bell and had the price of spot juice up 12 cents a pound by 10:00 a.m. Every one cent move on a contract was worth $150.00. Kepler had been keeping track of the numbers. They had bought over 1500 contracts and were still buying. They had over $2 million in paper profits and the market was still moving higher!

Cecil remembered Kevin stepping into the pit and selling, or "going short," 100 contracts, watching the market fall 2 cents, then buying them back for a quick profit of $30,000.00. He remembered Kepler then doing the same thing again a few minutes later and making 3 cents instead of two. $45,000.00. Cecil was impressed.

He remembered walking into the center of the pit and selling fifty contracts and the market immediately moved up four cents, the two strangers buying all they could. $30,000.00 in the hole and Cecil didn't cut loss. He decided to stay with the position. He remembered looking over at Kepler and seeing his face, grimacing, maybe trying to tell him to get out. Then, the market jumped up another $22,500.00. Cecil remembered standing there, looking over at Kepler, who was now smiling. Over $50,000.00 in the hole, and he was smiling.

Cecil had about eighty thousand in his account, his membership was worth thirty, and his new house on Long Island was worth three hundred, minus a mortgage of two hundred and fifty. Cecil felt comfortable, almost relaxed, as he sold fifty more contracts and watched Kepler's smile vanish immediately and right then the bells on the Reuters news wire began to ring. The runners began to read the news off the wire service and send messages back to the pit. Cecil looked around for his own runner and couldn't find him. Kepler began to walk towards him and he remembered the look on his face when he told him that the initial estimate of damage by the Florida Citrus Association was 75 million boxes, two thirds of the crop! And he remembered the next time he looked up at the price for Jan. juice it was another 20 cents higher. HE HAD JUST LOST ANOTHER $300,000. And he was still in the trade! He felt dizzy, nauseous, disoriented, as though he were about to pass out. Somehow he brought it all back together enough to buy back his 100 contracts about thirty cents above where he had sold them. He was down over $400,000. He had lost everything and where was Kepler. There he was. Smiling again. The market was still going up and Cecil had climbed out of the pit. Eight years of hard work and careful planning, gone in an instant. And still, after everything he had left was gone, he would still owe a quarter of a million to the exchange. And Kepler was smiling.

Cecil stared out into the ocean towards this hurricane that was coming and smiled to himself, deeply, and with great satisfaction. He was proud of himself, he had finally begun to even things up. And that, he smiled at the darkening sky, that was just the beginning.

Cecil got in his car and started it, put it in reverse, and slowly backed out of the driveway. He could picture the scene at the Fratino's house. It was the same thing every Sunday night. Had been for the last fifteen years. Kathy, his wife, and her mother, and Louis and Cecil. The smell of the spaghetti sauce was noticeable from the street in good weather when the windows were left open. This day qualified as a closed window day at the Fratino's. The wind was stronger than usual.

As Cecil drove into Brooklyn, he felt a sickening feeling he seldom felt anymore, a feeling of remorse that had first come over him ten years ago, after making an illegal business transaction with some of Fratino's friends, a transaction that had provided him with enough money to pay off the New York Cotton Exchange's collection attorneys. But all in all, a deal that had sickened him terribly. Not so much because of the illegality involved. It had more to do with the fact that never again would he be able to be his own man, and, once again, he would have to accept some intimidation in his life, and, at times, even some humiliation.

That night while Kathy said grace at the dinner table, and Cecil glanced around the table lit only by candlelight (the electricity had gone out just before dinner was served), his mind was no more at ease than was his white wrought iron patio furniture, which, at that very moment, was being seized by one of the hurricane's stronger, uncaring arms, and thrown violently through the big bay window of Cecil's empty living room on Long Island, allowing more than one large sliver of broken plate glass to come to rest, ominously, in the torn lime green uphol-stery of a certain overstuffed chair.

CHAPTER 4

When Mike woke up on Monday morning, the electricity was still out. It had gone out Sunday afternoon as the hurricane passed along the Eastern Shore of Maryland on its way north. He had driven back from Ocean City late the night before. As he had approached Annapolis, still some five miles east of the Chesapeake Bay Bridge, he noticed the absence of light. As he crossed the Narrows Bridge, which connects Kent Island to the mainland, everything was dark. Although it was late at night, things were darker than usual. As he crossed the Chesapeake Bay Bridge, the toll booths on the western side were lit by the power from a generator and they flickered on and off as the current fluctuated, giving off an iridescent glow in the otherwise blackened night. As he climbed out of bed now, he saw his digital clock radio still not showing a time.

He reached for the phone on the nightstand next to his bed, picked up the receiver, and heard no dial tone. He walked into the bathroom and turned on the hot water tap of the sink, filled his left palm with Gillette Foamy and then allowed his right hand to lash about under the faucet waiting for the cold water to warm. Of course, it didn't. He glanced over at the bathroom window and was glad it was there. Without it he would be shaving by candlelight. Finally realizing that the water would not be getting hot, he splashed the cold water on to his face and began to shave. He thought of Virginia and the thought of her made him smile.

The storm had done little damage to Toby's boat. When Mike left the hotel bar at nine o'clock the night before, Toby, Ben, and Osborn were totally wasted and planning on sleeping it off on the boat, now that the water had calmed and the storm had passed. Mike toweled off the excess lather from his face, glanced at the shower stall, and decided to take a quick cold shower.

After showering and dressing for work, he walked downstairs to the kitchen and poured himself a bowl of Raisin Bran. The milk from the refrigerator was still somewhat cool and he sat down at his table to eat, looking out his kitchen window at the beautiful sunny day. How strange it was, he reflected, that only yesterday afternoon things had been so loud, dark, and violent outside; now it was so calm, warm, and quiet.

After eating, he left for the office. His green MG glistened in the sun, still wet with drops and tiny puddles of rainwater from the night before. As he drove down Charles Street and turned on to Duke of Gloucester, he reached up and released the two latches that held the black vinyl top. His right arm lowered the top as his left arm stayed on the wheel. The temperature was in the 70's and the radio was playing a new song by Springsteen. He began to sing along.

His office was located on King George Street, on the west side of town, and he was there in ten minutes. He entered the left side entrance of an old, yellow, two story Victorian house which was his office. He leased the entire left side of the building though he only used the lower level. He had plans of one day converting the up-stairs to a large group therapy room, yet after three years of thinking about it, it remained only a plan.

Nancy Milkwood, his receptionist for the last five years, was already there, seated behind the desk. She was in her late twenties, a redhead, and as vivacious as one could ever imagine. All of the blinds were raised to the top of the windows and sunlight filled the office.

"No power!" Nancy said, holding her arms up in a helpless gesture.

"I know," Mike responded.

"How was the fishing?" she asked.

"You wouldn't believe it."

"I told you it was crazy going out there with that storm coming," she admonished him.

"I know, I know. And ordinarily I would say you were right."

"What do you mean?" She looked at him inquiringly, a serious expression on her freckled face. He told her about the weekend, the rescue, the hospital, and nothing about his feelings for Virginia. "You seem awfully happy. Doesn't really sound very enjoyable to me. Especially the part about the rolling and tossing waves, ugh!" She was referring to her own weak stomach and her utter lack of interest in boating.

"You would have been fine. All in your head." Mike pointed to her head and smiled before changing the subject.

"Who's up first?"

Nancy looked down at the calendar, then back to Mike, "Good old Mr. Rodriguez."

Rodriguez had been a patient for years and suffered from extreme anxiety, bordering on paranoia, about the fidelity of his wife. He was sure she was cheating on him regularly. "Good old Mr. Rodriguez." Mike smiled and walked into his office, closing the door behind him.

He sat back in his brown leather recliner and put his feet up on the desk, an old desk from the early 1900's he had purchased at an auction last summer. Nancy had already raised the blinds and opened both of his office windows a few inches, allowing a warm breeze to blow through his office, bringing in with it the sweet, wet smells of the flowers, shrubs, and earth outside.

He thought of Virginia. Her red hair was a deep, dark red, not the bright reddish orange color of Nancy's. Her skin was soft and fair, and not covered with the freckles one might expect to find. And those eyes, her beautiful dark brown eyes. And her laugh, her laugh had been like music. The breeze coming through the room was nudging him into a semi-sleep when suddenly he was jolted by a knock on his office door and the sound of it opening. Nancy was leading in an extremely tired and frightened looking Mr. Rodriquez.

"Sorry, no buzzer," Nancy offered as she entered. "Sit right over here, Mr. Rodriguez."

Mike was brought back to reality. "Good morning, Ernie. How are you doing?" Then looking back to Nancy, "Thanks, Nancy," as she was leaving the room and closing the door.

His session with Rodriguez blended in with three other patients that morning and by lunch time he remembered little about the sessions. His mind refused to find anything but Virginia to focus on, and he was enjoying it.

The electricity was still out at noon when Marcia, Mike's fiancée, walked in the door to greet him. He felt totally disoriented, as though he were watching a movie. He knew she could sense something was wrong but he didn't care. In fact, his smiling was bringing him more trouble than anything he said. It was mostly just his damn smile, and she told him so.

Marcia was in her mid-thirties, had light brown hair that fell to her shoulders in waves, and light blue eyes. She had a terrific figure, though at times, undressed, or in a bathing suit, Mike felt her thighs were a little too thick. She wore brown tortoise shell glasses when she read, and when she was not reading she kept them on a thin leather necklace that bounced around on her well developed breasts. As she spoke to Mike now, her glasses were motionless against a tight, gray sweater she was wearing under a blue blazer.

"So, Buster. What are you smiling about? I'll give you something to smile about." She turned to lock his office door in mid sentence. "I missed you." She began to move towards him.

"I was only gone for two days," Mike countered.

She walked up to his desk and knelt down beside him. Her hands came to rest on his belt buckle as she stared up at him mischievously. He stared down at her and brought her face up close to his and kissed her. She kissed him hard and passionately, saying "God, I love you so much," and waited for his response.

Mike hesitated before replying, "Love you too."

"So, how about lunch?" She stood up and her face was flushed.

Mike was smiling again now, "Sounds good to me." he said. "But no one has power back yet?"

Marcia leaned over and whispered into Mike's ear, "Serving at my place," gently blowing into his ear, her left breast pressing firmly against his chest.

"Let's go," Mike said as he stood up and ran his hand down over the front of his slacks.

As they walked out Mike asked Nancy for the time of his next appointment, thinking to himself, somewhat disgruntled, how damn reliable psychologically disturbed people were about keeping their appointments with their therapists regardless of what else might be happening.

"Two o'clock, a Mr. Cory," Nancy answered him. "Going for lunch, you think places are open?"

"My place is always open to this guy." Marcia put her arm around Mike as they began to leave.

"I think I'll just walk over to the deli," Nancy said, as though she were talking to herself, even though they were still in the room.

"See you later," Mike said as they walked out the door. The name Mr. Cory was unfamiliar to him, meaning it must be a new patient. He gave it little thought as he and Marcia climbed into his MG and headed for her place.

Mike thought about Virginia very little during or after lunch. He arrived back at his office shortly before two o'clock. He was even beginning to feel quite whimsical about it all. He entered his office through a side door and didn't see Richard Cory sitting patiently in the waiting room. When Nancy knocked on his door to announce this Mr. Cory, Mike wasn't as composed as he liked to be when meeting new patients for the first time.

"Mr. Cory is here?" Nancy said as she led him in to have a seat.

He was about thirty-five, very thin, and of medium height. His hair was black and fell loosely around his collar. His receding hairline was emphasized even more dramatically then usual because his hair appeared to be still damp. It was brushed back further and tighter than it ordinarily would be, as though he had just recently washed it. He wore a black, long sleeved t-shirt with some unintelligible silver markings on the front. His blue jeans were old and faded, and it wasn't until he stood to leave an hour later that Mike noticed a small silver patch of some sort sewn to his left trouser leg on the back. Richard Cory sat down and pulled out a green and white pack of Export A cigarettes and a box of wooden matches from his pocket.

"Mind if I smoke?" He chuckled, grinning nervously.

"That's fine, please. Let me just get you an ashtray." Mike kept a small glass ashtray in his right desk drawer. He kept it in the drawer to discourage smoking, yet he actually didn't mind so much.

He handed the ashtray to Mr. Cory. "Do I detect an accent? Canadian?" Mike inquired.

"Yes, you do. Toronto."

"Beautiful city."

"The good parts, certainly."

"Well, anyway. What may I do for you?" Mike was as ready as he would ever be.

"I've got a serious problem and I need help. I suppose you might diagnose me as a case of clinical depression."

"You feel depressed?"

"Very much so, at times. Most times actually. I've been to therapy before, you know. A long, long time ago." He exhaled the smoke from his cigarette with obvious pleasure, as though he truly enjoyed his smoking.

"For depression?"

"Yes. And anxiety. And insomnia. And..." he paused, "a whole rash of things, actually."

Mike settled back in his chair and asked, "And you feel like I might be able to help you?" Without getting more than a nod in response, Mike continued, "Well, why don't you tell me about yourself?"

"It's a long sad story, I'm afraid," Cory began, "and I'm not quite sure where to begin. Love is probably a good place to start, perhaps not the best place to start, but a good place nonetheless."

"Love?" Mike prompted him.

"Yes. I suffer from a sheer lack of love. Not the sort of loveless loneliness that most people experience at one time or another. Rather, a lack of love from having once had a great deal of it and now having it all gone, taken away from me in dribs and drabs over the years. I write about it, to myself, in a journal, yet it does no good. I seem to feel worse and worse as time marches on." He spoke with great concentration, as though he had rehearsed everything he was saying. "It hurts so much more to be without love once you have known it so well. At least, it seems that way, doesn't it? I mean, for those lonely creatures out there who have never even known the feeling of being loved, I'm sure it's painful, even quite awful, at times. But it certainly doesn't come close to matching the feeling of having it all taken away. It couldn't possibly. Anyway, I suppose I got an adequate amount of love from my family as a child, perhaps even more than most. I was showered with their pride and admiration. Honor student, skipping a grade in school, that sort of thing, you know. Well, they decided to disown me at the age of fifteen all because I decided to hit the road and see the world one summer rather than attend a Latin camp they had picked out for me. I moved all over the place. Canada and the states, met lots of people, made many friends, at least, they appeared to be friends. Wrote a lot of poetry, very good poetry too! Played the guitar, wrote my own music. I suppose I was finding myself, as they say. Anyway, from that point on my parents basically wrote me off. Oh, they would see me on holidays if I happened to call up for a visit, but that was about it. I traveled for four years, even made it to Europe one summer."

Mike interrupted him, curious, "And how did you manage to support yourself, to pay for all this traveling?" He was surprised, and pleased, that this Cory fellow had such an interesting story to tell.

"Mostly dealing. You know, small stuff. Lids, hash, acid. No great quantities, just enough to keep myself going. This was back in the late 60's, you know. Things were a lot different than now."

"Oh, I remember the sixties," Mike smiled, "I remember reading about people like you in *Time Magazine* and seeing you standing along stretches of open highway, hitchhiking all over the place. I envied you, you know."

Cory smiled and pointed a finger to Mike as he spoke, "So you were one of those bastards who would never pick us up?" He was kidding and it went over very well with Mike.

"You're right," Mike said as he laughed. "I wanted to on occasion but never did."

"Well, back to my story, after struggling through several painful love affairs in my early twenties, I fell in love with a close friend's wife. I just, well, I simply adored her. My friend suspected something was going on, but it wasn't. I'd never even told her how I felt. Then one day my friend woke up, drove out to the countryside, and drove his car over a cliff. Apparently she had been having an affair with someone else and he thought it was me. But it wasn't! My first therapy came at about that time."

"You haven't told me much about her?" Mike asked, "You say you loved her but never told her?"

"There was an awful lot going on in my life back then. I mean, I was taking a lot of acid," Richard explained.

"LSD?" Mike asked, "What's a lot?"

"Sometimes two or three times a day. I took too much. Ended up on the receiving end of a thorazine drip."

"What happened?" Mike's tone of voice became more serious, more professional.

"Well, I felt responsible for his death, I guess. Meanwhile she had run off with her lover. I took about fifteen tabs and a bunch of downers. I was in the hospital for a month. I had to learn to talk all over again. Write, too. But I made it." Cory paused, lighting another cigarette.

"So," he began again, "as you can see, a lot going on up here, wouldn't you say?" He pointed to his head.

Mike smiled and tried not to let his concern show. He knew what that much LSD could have done to the brain and he also knew that regardless of how good a job he did as a therapist he would never actually know where one road ended and another one began. Richard Cory. Wasn't there a poem? About a Richard Cory going home and putting a bullet through his head?

"Wasn't there a poem about—" Mike began to ask.

"Yes. And a song too, by Simon and Garfunkel." Cory paused, shifting restlessly in his chair. "Think you can help? Or does it all sound like too much for you?"

Mike took on a friendly, informal attitude. "Of course I think I can help. I know I can help, if you want it." Mike paused, then asked, "What brings you to Annapolis?"

"Love." Cory's expression was matter-of-fact. Then he smiled, broadly. "Can you believe it?"

"What's she like?" Mike asked.

"She's forty seven," Cory answered, "And she's still very hot."

"Tell me about her," Mike continued.

"Met her in New York, a widow. Her name is Rebecca Clemenzi. She came on to me at a poetry reading in the Village. I'm staying with her, she lives in Annapolis." Cory seemed eager to explain as much as he could about himself in the hour he had to work with, but his time was up. As Mike stood up to say goodbye he told him he really looked forward to working with him. Mike was sincere; he really liked this guy. And he hadn't once thought of Virginia.

The rest of the day included a marriage counseling session and a trip to Crownsville Hospital to visit a failed suicide. Later that evening, as he was driving back from Crownsville, most of the electricity was restored to the residents of Anne Arundel County. The five minute traffic lights at West Street and Route 2 were back in operation. As Mike sat at the light, barely even aware of it, he tried to come up with all of the many reasons why he should forget about Virginia and continue with his life, as he had left it on Friday. He knew he should be driving over to Marcia's apartment, where she would be waiting for him, ready to either go out or eat in, whatever he felt like doing. And when the honking of a horn behind him brought him out of his trance, he wasn't sure whether he should to turn at the light or keep going straight, even though he had come back home this way many times before.

CHAPTER 5

Virginia spent two nights at Johns Hopkins Hospital before she was well enough to be released. The doctor that initially examined her when Kevin brought her in had remarked about how well she seemed to be doing, considering what she had been through.

Kevin had slept fitfully Sunday night in a nearby hotel room he had taken to be close to the hospital. He had said goodbye to Bill and Joe about six o'clock and thanked them for their help. He had stayed in the hospital room with Virginia until about eight o'clock when he got a call from Megan. She was calling from her sister's house in Towson to check on Virginia and also to find out when she could come visit her. Kevin told her he was going to stay close to the hospital and suggested she come over in the morning. He told her to pack an overnight bag and confirmed that she would be leaving Jimmy and her father at her sister's house.

The following morning Virginia seemed to be feeling better. Seeing this, Kevin felt good about leaving her in the hospital for another day. He told her he would call her the next day. He said he had some things to take care of. Megan had just arrived and Kevin had made arrangements for her to stay the night in Virginia's private room, where a small roll-away bed had been set up in the corner near the window.

On Tuesday morning, after briefly talking to Kevin on the phone, Megan checked Virginia out of the hospital and by lunch time they were pulling into the main entrance of the ranch. Very little was said on the trip down, not so much because Virginia didn't feel like talking, but more so because she didn't really have a whole lot she wanted to say to Megan. Since Megan had accepted Christ as her savior it had been quite difficult to talk with her about anything without having the subject turn to Jesus. It wasn't that talk of Jesus, or Christianity, really bothered Virginia all that much. Sometimes she actually enjoyed it. It was just with the shock of losing Nathan still fresh in her mind she really didn't want to talk about salvation. She was grieving and wanted to be left alone with her grief. Of course, if she had been with someone else on the drive down, for instance, her father, it would have been easier to talk about it. But with Megan, a warm silence had been nice.

Once up in her room, which was on the second floor of the spacious colonial style home, she felt much better.

This was her home. She had grown up here. She had gone through school here, just a few miles away. Her bedroom reflected ten years of warmth and love, some pain and bad memories, but mostly a life full of good times.

A picture of her natural mother, Liz, caught her eye as she walked into the room. It hung on the wall beside her dresser as it had for a decade. Virginia walked over to the picture and looked at it carefully, slowly, and actually for the first time in a long time she looked at the picture and remembered what her mother had been like, how happy she had been, how happy her father had been, and how painful it had been to lose her when they did.

Her eyes moved across the top of her dresser and came to rest on a picture of Nathan, standing proudly beside his favorite mare, in front of the stables, smiling at her, the woman he loved, the woman he wanted to spend the rest of his life with. Virginia began to weep, though it was a contained kind of crying, a healthy weeping that felt good. She smiled through her tears as she walked over to the window and looked out over the vast green fields and hills that seemed to stretch as far as she could see.

As her eyes dried she began to notice the familiar sounds of the ranch, the neighing of the horses and the occasional buzzing of a confused fly trying to get through the screen. She noticed the familiar smells, from the fragrance of the flowers below her window to the manure across the yard in the stables, and she felt glad to be home. She was anxious to see her father soon. She hadn't seen him since Monday morning and she knew how concerned and worried he had been, and she knew he was out there trying to feel more at ease about what had happened. But she knew, she could tell from the sound of his voice on the phone the night before when he had called to check up on her, that he was still shaken. He was thinking about how close he had come to losing her, and she knew how much it must have hurt him. As she looked again over at the picture of her mother on the wall and thought of how much love she felt for her father, the tears began to come again, though this time they represented joy rather than sorrow.

She walked over to her canopy bed to lie down. The warm autumn breeze gently blowing in through her window felt gentle and loving against her face. She closed her eyes and let her thoughts flow freely and quite soon she fell asleep.

She was awakened by the sound of the telephone ringing in the distance, knowing it was coming through the walls and down the hall from her father's room. As she looked over at her own telephone, which was a different line than her parent's phone, she smiled, knowing it was her father calling and knowing he had chosen to call on the other line in case she was sleeping. She jumped up and was surprised at the dizzy, lightheaded feeling which came over her. She was more aware of her weakened state as she waited a moment for her head to steady before standing up to walk downstairs.

At the top of the stairway she could hear Megan's voice talking from the kitchen below, and she could tell from the sound of her voice she was talking to Kevin. By the time she reached the bottom of the stairs she heard her saying goodbye. She walked into the big, open kitchen and noticed by the clock on the wall that it was a little after four o'clock.

"Oh," said Megan, seeing Virginia walk in, "that was your father. He'll be home for dinner about six. Feeling a little better?"

"Yea." Virginia smiled, adding, "I'm okay. I'm glad Dad is coming home."

"I know you are sweetie," Megan said, continuing, "I think you worry about him sometimes as much as I do, God bless you."

"Megan?" Virginia started.

"Yes."

"I'm still a little foggy about a few things."

"Like what?"

"Oh, like what day it is for starters."

They both laughed together. "I mean, was yesterday Monday? The day you drove the Hollingsworths back to Fenwick, was that yesterday?"

"Let me see." Megan was searching her memory. "Yes. Monday. I was supposed to take them back home before I came to see you at the hospital. But they just loved the hotel your father put them up in and decided to stay one more night in Baltimore. Your father drove them back to Fenwick today. Why are you asking?"

"Well, wasn't Dad acting a little strange about things? I mean, he acted like he wanted them to come and stay on the ranch with us, or was I just groggy?"

"No, I think you're right, come to think of it. But I think he was tired, too. We were all so tired from that cursed storm. Can you believe that storm? My goodness gracious. Two hundred mile an hour winds by the time it was over!"

"Yea, it was a lot stronger than they first said it would be." She began to think about Saturday morning at Fenwick when she and Nathan had decided to go sailing. They had listened to the weather report on Friday night reporting a small tropical storm still hundreds of miles away. She began to feel lightheaded again and walked towards the white oak dinette table in the center of the breakfast room to sit down. Her movement indicated she was feeling a little shaky and Megan began to walk towards her just as she started to fall.

When she regained consciousness she was back upstairs in her bedroom again, in bed, wearing her nightgown. Kevin sat in a chair right beside her.

"Dad?" she began, "Oh Dad, I'm so glad to see you." She reached out and hugged him tightly. "I can't believe it. I've never fainted before, can you?"

Kevin's ordinarily hard, determined countenance was now twisted up into a face of deep caring and love. "Dr. Bacon came by and said you were going to be just fine." She could sense the hidden worry in his voice again. "He said you ought to stay in bed the rest of the week and he left some medicine for you." Kevin indicated a small medicine bottle on her bedside table. "Now that you're awake let's take one." He reached for the bottle, opened it, and handed her a pill with her water glass.

"What is it?" Virginia asked, reaching for the bottle and then reading the label. "Valium!" she exclaimed. "You're kidding, aren't you?"

"Please, just take them for a couple of days. You've been through so much." His face had taken on a puppy like quality as he asked her to take the pill.

"For you, Dad. But I don't really need a tranquilizer." She swallowed the pill and set the glass back down on her nightstand. "I wanted so much to have dinner with you tonight, downstairs."

"Dr. Bacon says the stress can cause lightheadedness, even fainting. That's why he wants you to take these. So, please, for me. You'll take 'em?"

"Yes, I'll take them," she sighed. "You probably ought to take one too, Dad," she kidded him, "you look like you could use it."

"Very funny," he replied, "now you just relax and try to sleep. I'll be here in the morning." He stood up and said, "How about a date for breakfast, say, nine o'clock? Just you and me? Right here?" He was smiling down at her.

"Sure Dad. Wouldn't miss it," she responded, "stay with me awhile tonight though?"

"You got it." He sat back down again and gave her a warm smile.

II

Megan sat alone at the white oak table while Kevin sat with Virginia upstairs. She was trying not to wring her hands, trying to relax, trying to pray. Yet, her mind simply insisted on replaying the scene in the kitchen from earlier that day.

She had noticed some unsteadiness in Virginia's gait, and she had even managed to catch her before she hit the floor. Those few minutes that Virginia had been unconscious had really scared her. "Thank the Lord!" she thought to herself. "And thank God Bertha was here." Bertha, the family maid, had been there to get her through it, had been the one to tell her to use ammonia on a rag under the nose if she had to. And after trying a cold wash cloth which didn't work, she had to use the ammonia. The smell on the rag had been horrible. But Bertha had gotten her through it, not the Lord, but Bertha. And thank God Pete had not gone home yet, good old Pete, who had cleaned the stables, maintained the lawn, and cared for the horses the last ten years. Thank God he was still there to help get Virginia back up the stairs and into her bed. Thank God for Pete.

"Oh when will he ever come down here?" Her mind continued to race. "Will he ever come down at all? Or will he spend the night up there in her room?" Then, speaking out loud, she began to pray. "Oh Lord, please give me the strength to get through these anxious moments, give me the peace of mind to find the time to fully appreciate my love for you, the insignificance of my own problems when compared to the suffering you went through before you died, all alone and in such pain, with such love, on a cross. Oh Lord, let me just take these trying times as easily as I can, and get through this night, with your love. Through Jesus Christ my lord, Amen." She immediately felt better, finishing her prayer, yet her mind continued to race.

She was still sitting quietly at the table, still trying not to wring her hands, when Kevin entered the room.

Having not heard his footsteps coming downstairs, she was startled. "Oh, Kevin," she said as she stood up and rushed up to him, embracing him desperately.

"What's this? Relax, will you?" He paused and looked over at the tea kettle on the stove. "How about some hot chocolate? We'll drink it out back on the porch." His voice was soothing.

"And look at the stars?" Megan's eyes were glistening from her tears as she gazed lovingly into his eyes, asking him for much more than to share a hot cocoa on the patio. And as he looked back at her, he knew it.

"And look at the stars," he said, kissing her on the forehead as he began to move towards the stove. "I know this has been difficult for you. And I appreciate you being here." He still looked at her as he said this.

"I love you, Kevin Kepler, much more than I probably should love someone but I just can't help it, and you know it. Now get out of the way," she exclaimed, "and let me make the cocoa!" She gently pushed him away from the stove as she spoke.

"I love you too, Meg." Kevin walked over and sat down at the table and they both said nothing as they waited for the water to boil.

When the hot chocolate was ready they both walked out on to the back porch, a wide verandah that encircled half the house. Kevin sat down in an old, white rocking chair that needed painting, and Megan sat across from him on the railing that ran along the edge of the porch. They said very little to each other, not that Megan didn't want to talk. Kevin was obviously enjoying the quiet of the night, the occasional sound of chirping crickets, and the piece of mind in knowing that his daughter slept soundly, if not completely well, upstairs.

Their home was set back several hundred yards from the main road. From where Kevin was sitting on the porch, he was staring out towards the two red brick columns at the driveway entrance. Very little traffic ran up and down this particular stretch of road since the new state highway had been completed a few miles to the east several years ago. When the sound of a passing car was heard at all, it drew little attention. But this evening, when a passing set of headlights slowed suspiciously, almost coming to a complete halt near the main gate, Kevin noticed it. And when the car slowly started to move again, almost passing the property without being seen or heard, he knew it was there.

III

The next morning Virginia was rousted out of a deep sleep by her favorite person in the whole world, next to her Dad. Bertha, their housekeeper. Bertha had been with the family since they first got to Virginia. Bertha was short, about five feet high, and a little on the heavy side. Her skin was a dark shade of brown, all but the palms of her hands. Her black hair was short, or seemed to be, and she constantly wore a small black cap over the top of her head as part of her starched white uniform. Once, when Virginia was about seven, she had seen Bertha without her cap, and it was hard to tell for sure about the length of her hair because of the abundance of bobby pins. Bertha's smile was heartfelt, her laugh deep and totally ingenuous. A warm kindness emanated from her voice when she spoke, even when she tried to sound menacing or threatening when upset about something. She was unique and adorable and loved by everyone. When Virginia awoke to the sound of Bertha's voice that morning, she was filled with happiness. The valium haze cleared as soon they began to speak.

"Wake up, girl," Bertha began. "Your Daddy be up here directly." The 'i' in her "directly" rhymed with pie, and much emphasis had been given to the word 'wake'.

"Bertha, oh I'm so glad to see you. Did you hear about what—" she began to ask.

"I heard." Bertha's face was warm, yet she was scowling. "You had no business bein' out in that storm, young lady."

"I know, but it just didn't sound like it was gonna be that bad. Honest." Virginia apologized.

"Uh-huh." This is what Bertha would say when she meant 'Sure you did'. She turned to walk over and open the curtains all the way and raise the shade.

"No, really. You should have heard the forecast. They said a small tropical depression was about three hundred miles east of some place in South Carolina. Friday night!"

Bertha turned towards her to speak, hands on her wide hips, "And you figured that the followin' mornin' you'd go sailin' out there. Don't you think those tropical dee-pressions move overnight? Or you figure they just stay in one place? What am I going to do with you, girl?" She walked over and stood beside the bed. "Now let's be gettin' up and washed before your Daddy gets up here."

She offered to help, "You want to get up and wash your face, you need to use the commode? Let me help you, girl. Here, now, steady." She helped Virginia out of bed and into the bathroom.

"Bertha," Virginia asked, before closing the bathroom door all the way.

"What is it?" Bertha answered.

"Think you could stay with us a few days, overnight I mean?"

"I'll overnight you!" Bertha exclaimed. "Close that door and do your business. Your daddy be up here directly." She began to move towards the door, then hesitated. "You let me know when you're done, I'll be right here." A look of concern covered Bertha's face yet the tone of her voice was jovial.

Kevin knocked softly and opened the door behind Bertha. "How is she?" he asked as he entered.

"She's in the bathroom. She'll be fine, don't you worry," Bertha responded, almost whispering, then loudly she announced, "Your daddy's here girl, you about ready?"

The sound of the flushing toilet and the running water of the sink came through the closed bathroom door. After a few moments the door opened and Virginia appeared, looking wide awake and very beautiful. "Morning, Dad."

"Good morning," said Kevin, who then turned and said to Bertha, "well, we're ready?"

"Let me get myself downstairs and I'll be right back up with it." She scurried out of the room, repeating herself, "I'll be right back," on the way out.

"So," began Kevin, "feeling better?"

Virginia walked over to the window as she answered him, feeling the light breeze press up against her nightgown, "Much," and took a deep breath of fresh air before turning around to face him. "Dad?" she began.

"Yes," Kevin said as he moved towards her.

"What are Nathan's parents going to do about a funeral?" She seemed as though she had thought this out completely before asking.

"A private service is planned for Saturday, in Richmond, but I don't think you..." he paused. "I told his father we'd all be there in sympathy. I think that will be just fine. And he agreed." Kevin sounded as though his mind were made up and Virginia could tell by the way he was talking that he didn't want her to go, that he wanted her to stay right here and get better.

"But don't you think," she began to protest and suddenly stopped. "I guess you're right." She moved towards the bed and reached for the bottle of valium on the night stand and took one out.

"Here," said Kevin, reaching for the water glass, "let me get you some fresh water."

"Dad," she asked as he was filling her glass in the bathroom.

"Yea?" he answered loudly, then turned off the water and walked back into her room. "What is it?"

She was back in bed now, covers pulled up over her legs to her stomach, her head propped up on a couple of pillows. "That guy, Mike?"

"Yea?"

"I mean, you did thank him and everything I'm sure. It's just..." she stopped as if thinking.

"Just what?" he asked.

"Oh nothing," she answered, just as Bertha entered the room with a tray, holding their breakfast in both hands, balancing the tray so as to not spill a thing.

Bertha set the tray down on a small, round table in the corner of the room and Kevin sat down in a chair next to the bed. Virginia, with the gentleness of the Valium just beginning to kick in, watched her two most favorite people in the world while she smiled in anticipation of the good breakfast Bertha had prepared. Bertha left the two of them alone to eat and walked back downstairs. She found Megan seated alone out on the porch, drinking her morning coffee and watching the day begin. Without giving her a second thought, Bertha moved towards the laundry room, where her first load of wash had just finished spinning.

The following day was a little better for Virginia, her lightheadedness having not returned to bother her again. After showering and dressing, she walked downstairs to the kitchen where she found Bertha polishing some silverware over the sink. The smell of the silver polish, though it was quite strong, filled Virginia's nostrils and she smiled, feeling good all over about being home. She announced to Bertha that she was going to take a walk over to the stables to see the horses. Especially her own horse, Jonathan.

Bertha tried to prevent her from going outside, but finally sighed, shaking her head in dismay, and simply said, "What am I gonna do with you, girl?"

Virginia spent the rest of the day wandering in and out of the house, restlessly. Except for a brief conversation she had with Bertha while eating her lunch at the kitchen table about whether or not it was okay for her to go riding, she spoke with no one else until Kevin and Megan returned from a visit to see Nathan's parents in Richmond.

The next day, Friday, Kevin came upstairs to say goodbye to her and apologized for having to go away for the weekend. He assured her that he would be back as early as possible Saturday night. He didn't tell her where he was going and she didn't ask. She knew it must have been important and she also knew how much he needed his little secrets. He told her Bertha would stay over for the weekend and that was more than enough to please her. She thanked him, kissed him on the cheek, and tucked her head back comfortably into her pillow as she watched him walk out the door.

Staying so close to home had been more difficult than Kevin had imagined it would be. He was glad to be back out in the world again. As he drove down the highway towards the airport, he began to feel less worried about Virginia's health and more optimistic about her recovery. Although he felt bad thinking it, he was relieved she would not be getting married after all; she would be his little girl that much longer.

IV

He was on his way to a meeting in Bermuda. His family had recently sold some property over there to a syndicate of developers who were showing their appreciation by throwing a cocktail party at the Southampton Princess. He had given up, at least for the time being, on trying to find out who was behind the attack on his daughter. He even began to entertain the idea that it had been a freak accident of some sort. His contact at the Coast Guard station, Captain Shultz, had suggested in their last conversation that it could have been a much larger ship that struck the catamaran without even knowing it, perhaps a cargo vessel. After several days of toying with this unlikely possibility it was finally starting to make sense. As he drove towards the airport he was beginning to look forward to the weekend.

He was also feeling good because he was alone again. Originally, Megan was to have gone with him. But now, with Virginia still not right, she had offered to stay home to watch her, allowing Kevin to fulfill his obligation. And though he loved Megan, at times even quite intensely, he was now actually grateful to be by himself. He felt good about the fact that Pete had agreed to stay on over the weekend, and he knew that between Bertha, Pete, and Megan, his girl would be safe and well taken care of.

He arrived at the airport and boarded the DC-9. As he settled into the first class section, his mind began to wander back in time, to his first trip to Bermuda. As a young boy, he and his parents had traveled to Bermuda on one of those big elegant sea planes that had shuttled travelers back and forth for years before finally being stopped because the Second World War had begun. He still remembered the excitement of the takeoff as the engines roared loudly and the spray of the harbor's water splashed relentlessly over the small windows of the plane. The interior of the sea plane had been almost like a small, cozy, private club. People sat at tables and talked, playing gin rummy and drinking whiskey and seltzer from finely decorated tumblers. And he, a five year old boy full of wonder, had sat quietly next to his father, watching the water dance on the windows as the plane rose out of the harbor and into the air.

Now, as the DC-9 rose into the air, and everyone on board was held 'securely' by their seat belts, Kevin chuckled to himself before he opened his eyes and looked around. He looked at the passengers sitting across from him and in front of him before looking directly at the woman seated next to him.

He had noticed her when he first sat down but had let it go. She was attractive, a blond in her early thirties and well dressed. Now that he thought to notice, she wore a 3 or 4 carat diamond on her wedding finger. She spoke to him and he noticed an accent, either Swiss or Norwegian. "What is so funny?" she asked, referring to his chuckle.

"Oh, nothing," he responded.

"Oh," she said.

"I was just thinking about the old seaplanes that used to fly into St. George's," he explained.

"Seaplanes?" She sounded curious, obviously born a few years too late to know what he was talking about.

"Yea," he perked up a bit, "people used to fly to Bermuda in seaplanes. They were wonderful. No seat belts, people moving about freely after take off, and, except for the noise of the engines, a great way to travel."

"I prefer trains," she said, reaching for a pack of Parliament cigarettes in her purse. "Of course, that does me little good on a trip such as this!" she laughed.

"My name is Kevin, Kevin Kepler," he introduced himself.

"Rene Troyat," she offered her hand.

"French? But you sound…" he began.

"I know," she explained, "I grew up in Lucerne."

"It's beautiful there," he said, smiling.

"Indeed," she said.

They were silent now as she continued smoking her cigarette. By the time the plane landed at Bermuda International, she had agreed to share a taxi with Kevin to the Princess, where she had also been invited to a reception that evening.

Kevin's eyes lit up at the airport when he saw Johnny standing next to his taxi in the line of cabs waiting for passengers. Johnny was a well known cab driver on the island. He had been driving his cab for almost forty years, and between what he earned as a driver and what his wife managed to bring in, he had put all six of his children through college in the states. His pride in accomplishing this was evident when he shared the story with his passengers. Kevin had almost listened to the same story twice several years ago after some time had passed since first hearing it. But Johnny had recognized Kevin from before and laughed as he apologized for repeating himself. Since that time Kevin had ridden with him many times. Now, seeing him standing there in his colorful shirt and shorts, not showing the age of his sixty plus years at all, Kevin looked over to Rene and said, "We are in luck."

The Princess was about a twenty minute ride from the airport and Johnny brought Kevin up to date on the latest developments with his kids. As the entrance of the hotel finally came into view, and Johnny was expertly maneuvering his taxi through a cluster of mopeds, Kevin thought of the first time he stayed at the Princess as a young boy. He remembered when Johnny had first told him the story of the big, ugly hotel on a hill. About how the locals had always referred to it as a 'ghosthouse' because it had been built on top of an old cemetery. At night, Johnny had said, it even looked like a huge haunted castle perched menacingly on the hill overlooking the village of Hamilton. Young Kevin had barely slept his first night there.

Saying goodbye now to Johnny, then to Rene, Kevin carried his overnight bag with him through the sliding doors on his way over to a wall of telephones on the opposite end of the expansive lobby. His first call was to home to check on things. His second was to Fenwick Island, to Mrs. Hollingsworth, where, to his surprise, he got no answer. His third call was to Ocean City. When a voice answered "Boardwalk Copter Rides, Joe speaking," Kevin smiled to himself, reassured to hear the sound of a familiar voice, happy to have had the honor of knowing the person on the other end of the phone. He was anxious to find out what, if anything, Bill and Joe had discovered so far.

V

The reception that Rene attended that night happened to be the same party that the investor group had thrown in celebration of the deal they had closed with Kevin's father. Kevin was standing towards the front of the small ballroom, talking to one of the brothers involved in the deal, when he caught a glimpse of Rene standing near the buffet table. It was late in the evening and he was surprised that he hadn't noticed her earlier.

He began to make some effort at ending the trite conversation he was currently having and move on over across the room to say hello. After trying several times to end the investor's incessant babble about wine, Kevin abruptly excused himself and walked over towards Rene.

"So," she paused, "Hello again?" She was wearing a long flowing silver sequined evening gown and had made herself up to look even more beautiful than she had been on the plane.

"Hi, there," Kevin said, smiling. "You look beautiful," he commented, politely.

"Thank you," said Rene before sensually opening her mouth and closing it around a Swedish meatball, slowly withdrawing the toothpick out through glistening lips. "I am so sorry to have heard about your daughter. You must have been so afraid."

Kevin, who was rarely stunned or startled about anything, froze. He stared at her curiously, knowing she couldn't have known about it, or so he thought. He asked her, "How did you hear about it?"

"I simply heard it from someone," she replied.

"Really, who did you hear about it from?" Kevin asked.

"Why are you so alarmed? I simply thought it polite to ask about her. Certainly it must have been quite, shall we say, traumatic?" Rene sounded as though she was quite willing to change the subject with just the slightest provocation.

"I'm just concerned for her," Kevin explained.

"Of course you are," said Rene. "As a good papa should be." She smiled. "Shall we have a drink?"

"Of course, we should have a drink," Kevin responded as he moved with her towards the bartenders.

He was worrying now about things at an almost relentless pace. The thought of a glass of wine sounded soothing to him, though he seldom drank, and as they approached the long bar set up against the side wall he continued the conversation with her until they had ordered their drinks, at which time Rene took it upon herself to change the subject.

"So these people have bought some property from you?" she inquired innocently.

"From my father," Kevin answered. The wine was helping a little but he was still having a difficult time.

The soothing effect of the wine began to wear off rather quickly as Kevin's mind refused to focus in on the frivolous mood of the revelers around him. It made no sense to him that Rene should know about the incident with Virginia; it bothered him that his so typically private life had apparently become public. He was determined to find out who had been spreading the story.

"So, Rene," he began, "who told you about Virginia's accident?"

"Oh, Kevin. I thought you were not going to worry so much anymore. It was one of those two gentlemen standing over there by the door. They were flirting with me earlier and to get rid of them I mentioned I had come to the island with you, I hope you do not mind, though it is true, and they began to talk about your terrible misfortune. I was forced to pretend a knowledge of it so as to not appear totally ridiculous. Anyway, they left me alone and that was that. Why does it bother you so?"

Kevin was looking over at the two men by the door as Rene was explaining to him what had happened. He now looked back at her to excuse himself. "I'm going to go introduce myself." He set the wine glass down on a table and began to walk towards them. "I'll be right back," he said to her over his shoulder.

"Hello, my name is Kepler. Kevin Kepler. I hope you are enjoying yourselves?" His introduction left them no choice but to introduce themselves.

"So pleased to meet you, Mr. Kepler. My name is Bartiloni, Bernardo Bartiloni," began the older gray haired gentleman, "and this is my nephew Mark Canapele," he said as he introduced the younger man standing next to him. "I have been a friend of your mother for years. I am honored to finally meet you, having heard so much about you."

"Yea, that's why I wanted to come over and talk to you," Kevin said. "I understand you know about my daughter's accident last week. Did you hear about it through my mother?"

"Of course. I am so sorry to hear about it. I hope she will be okay?"

"She'll be fine. When did you talk to my mother?" Kevin continued.

"Oh," the older man paused to reflect. "Let me see. Was it maybe, yes, it was Monday morning. She called me on another matter. We were discussing the terrible storm and, well, she told me what happened. She is such a strong woman, your mother. You must be very proud?"

"Oh, I am," Kevin responded. "So, would you mind if I ask you to keep it to yourself awhile? At least until I know how my daughter's going to be? You know, the last thing we need are lots of phone calls and sympathy cards and flowers. You see what I mean?"

"Of course, I didn't even..." the older man began to apologize.

"I know. You didn't realize. But, please." Kevin asked of him again.

"Of course. Not another word." They shook hands and Kevin walked back over to where Rene was still standing near the side bar.

"Everything all taken care of?" she asked him, smiling in a concerned way.

"Yea, just fine." Kevin was more upset than he had been. "Listen, I'm going to go around, shake some hands, and say good night."

Rene glanced at her watch and remarked, "It is nearing twelve. Are you flying back in the morning?"

"Yea, first thing," he said. "Listen, it was wonderful meeting you. I hope you've had a good time."

"It was wonderful meeting you, too. I had hoped to see yet some more of you tonight. I am sorry I won't be able to." She looked genuinely disappointed.

"Well, I've got to be off. Goodbye, Rene."

"Goodbye Kevin. Until we meet again?"

"Au revoir," said Kevin as he turned and walked away. He walked into a crowd of people in the middle of the floor until he was out of her sight, and then walked straight towards the lobby. He had to try to reach Joe again. They should have had time to drive up to Fenwick and back again by now. He wanted to hear that the Hollingsworths were all right. He wanted to call his mother about this Bartiloni character. And more than anything else, he wanted to call home, even though it was so late. His shaken composure told him something was wrong and he was not sure where the feelings were coming from, though he knew he would soon find out.

When Kevin got to his room his mind was moving too fast and he knew he needed to slow it down before making any calls. He walked into the bathroom and washed his face with warm water before returning to the bedroom. He sat down on the bed closest to the sliding glass doors which opened on to the balcony. He loosened his tie, took off his shoes, leaned back on the bed, and closed his eyes. He could hear the sound of the ocean as the waves broke against the beach. He thought about moving the chair out to the patio yet decided against it.

He pictured an image of himself, dressed just as he was, standing out in the middle of a meadow of gently rolling hills and ankle deep grass. The sun was shining, high in the sky, and a few floating white clouds were moving slowly across the horizon. In the distance he saw a stand of trees, and off to the right a small stream. An old stone bridge ran across the stream. The stones were black and dark gray in color, though the bridge was too far away to notice any fine detail. Nothing else could be seen for miles around him; he was all alone. He could smell the fresh air, feel the grass around his stockinged feet, and in the distance he heard the sound of running water from the stream. Far above his head, from off to the left, he saw a hawk moving quietly, gliding effortlessly through the sky. Suddenly, the hawk's wings began to move up and down, propelling his flight, and he noticed the colors of the feathers were brown, red, and white. Then he became one with the hawk, gliding through the sky, moving his powerful wings slowly up and down as he watched the earth below. He felt no fear at all, only peace and power. He left the hawk, easily, returning to the meadow. He sat down in the grass. He could feel the dampness of the ground. He began to look around him. On the ground nearby was a large rock, an old weatherworn stone that looked as though it had been there forever. He gazed at the stone and let his mind wonder freely. No thoughts from his conscious mind found any room, an inner peace began to surface, and his eyes closed as he let himself be embraced by this feeling. He slowly began to drift off into sleep, his conscious mind giving way to the rushing, pulling arms of his deep subconscious, until soon he was fast asleep.

VI

As Kevin slept, back at Fenwick Island, Mr. and Mrs. Hollingsworth were both sitting upright in their bed. She was reading the latest Ludlum book and Donald had just switched off the news. He sat peacefully, his eyes closed, when he heard a loud sound from the other end of the house. Mrs. Hollingsworth looked at him quickly, fearfully, as he climbed out of bed and put on his slippers before opening the bedside table drawer for his flashlight. He walked around the bed, motioning with his hand for his wife to be quiet and stay put.

She watched him as he walked out the door and into the hall. He was keenly aware of how quiet it was out there. She didn't hear his shuffling feet, as she usually would, and she imagined that he must be walking very carefully, lifting one foot up and then the other so that he would make no noise. As soon as he was out of sight she began to tremble. The next few moments of silence were almost unbearable as she fought the inclination to get up herself and follow him out there. "If only," she thought to herself, "if only I'd listened to Kevin about keeping a gun in the house for protection. If only I hadn't been so thick skulled about it." Her arms and hands were shaking now, even before she heard the sound of a thud and the noise of Donald falling to the linoleum floor.

He was just walking into the kitchen when suddenly he was struck in the head from behind. Shortly after he fell, or possibly even as he was falling into unconsciousness, the piercing sound of Mrs. Hollingsworth's scream filled the small house. And just as her screaming was at its most shrill she heard the breaking glass of her bedroom window. Another loud sound came from the living room as the front door was nearly torn from its hinges. As the terror gripped her she closed her eyes and screamed even more loudly, louder than she thought possible. Gunfire, short and sporadic, shattered the pause left by a gasp in her screaming. As she pulled desperately on the covers she opened her eyes for only a second, quite by accident. She would have just as quickly shut them had she not recognized the person standing in the middle of her bedroom, tall and smiling, a 9mm pistol clasped tightly in his right hand and blood dripping from a cut on his forehead. Shattered panes of glass littered the floor. Bill's eyes darted quickly to hers and then back up to the door before looking back to her. He motioned for her to be quiet with his free hand. He then moved slowly around the bed towards the door. From the dark corridor of the hallway he heard another sound, a quick kicking, pounding sound. He reached over and turned off the light above Mrs. Hollingsworth's bed.

Her arms were still trembling, almost frantically, as she tried to breathe slowly, tried to be quiet. Another sound was heard from the other end of the house before a shouting voice was heard from the same direction saying, "Clear in here." Mrs. Hollingsworth's tense face eased somewhat upon hearing it.

"Clear in here too," Bill responded as he reached over and turned on the light above Mrs. Hollingsworth's bed, saying to her, "Be cool just one more minute." He walked out of the room and met Joe kneeling in the hall over Mr. Hollingsworth's body.

"He'll be okay, I think," said Joe. "I'll call the paramedics. How is she?"

"She's fine. Must have scared the hell out of her but she's fine," Bill answered as he moved towards the kitchen. "You did leave one of these bastards alive, didn't you?"

"Yea. Over there." Joe motioned towards a body lying in the corner of the living room. "He'll come to in a minute. Watch him while I call."

Bill moved over to stand near the guy just as Mrs. Hollingsworth shouted, "Bill? Is it okay? Is Donald —"

"You can come out here and see him. I think he'll be okay. I've gotta watch this other one here," Bill shouted to her from the living room.

She rushed out of her room and was by Donald's side in seconds, rubbing her hand across his forehead. She walked into the kitchen to wet a dishrag just as Joe was hanging up the phone.

"Evening Mrs. Hollingsworth." The sound of broken glass crackled under Joe's shoes. "Watch out for the glass. Sorry to bust things up like this but we had to get in quick."

"Thank God you were here," she said as she rushed back over to Donald's body applying the cool rag to his head. "How in the world?" she began. "What was this all about? I don't understand." She was shaking her head and rubbing Donald's forehead as she spoke.

"We had just driven down to check on you, as per instructions, and we happened to arrive at the right time," Joe offered.

"Joe." Mrs. Hollingsworth looked at him sternly. "How long were you two sitting out there?"

"Well," he began, just as Bill entered the room, "not long."

"Couple of hours," said Bill as he walked in. "I tied the scumbag up."

"And Kevin had you watch over us?" she asked.

"Well, sort of, he…" Joe began, before Bill interrupted him.

"He tried to call you earlier and you were gone. He called us. We drove down. No big deal." He looked around the room at the broken glass and wood on the floor. Bill smiled at Joe, saying, "Made a hell of a mess, didn't we?"

Joe looked around and shook his head in agreement before looking back up at Bill. "You want to call him or you want me to."

"You're the guy who wanted the brewskys," Bill responded, looking over towards Donald's body. Joe had insisted on running down to the store for a six-pack while they were watching the place from outside.

Joe looked at Bill, saying, "Yea, well I didn't hear you arguing about it."

"You're right. But I should've stayed here," Bill said as he walked over towards the telephone, repeating under his breath, "should've stayed here." As he dialed the number, with his back towards Mrs. Hollingsworth, he mouthed to Joe, "Fuck," and a pensive expression replaced his ordinarily resilient countenance as he waited for Kevin to answer the phone.

The sound of the ringing telephone startled Kevin out of a deep sleep. He answered the phone and listened carefully to Joe's report. Then he called the airline he had flown in on and booked a seat on the next flight back.

CHAPTER 6

Cecil began packing his matching, powder blue calf-skin suitcases. He had just received a call from Louis Fratino, telling him that Kepler had caught the two guys he had hired to attack Mr. and Mrs. Hollingsworth. Just recently, with the help of a private investigator, he had found out how close this old Hollingsworth couple was to Kevin. They were old and would have died soon anyway. He had paid Louis Fratino to have them killed and make it look like a random attack, maybe a burglary gone bad, just as he had paid him to create the boating accident.

Now that Kepler knew Cecil was behind it all, Cecil had no choice but to run, to run away fast. Far away, where no one could ever find him. He was sweating profusely although it was quite cool in the room. He looked around his bedroom, sadly, one last time before closing his bags. His wife would not be home until late in the afternoon. He would have to call her from somewhere on the road.

He put on his gold-rimmed sunglasses and looked at himself in the mirror. He looked fat, tired, and pathetic. He spent no time worrying about it as he moved quickly over to his dresser and put a handful of hundred dollar bills from his bureau into his pants pocket. From a lower drawer he reached for a 38 caliber revolver he had never fired and put it, along with a translucent plastic box of extra ammunition, into the pocket of his madras sport coat. He thought of leaving a note for Kathy but decided against it.

As he left the house through the side door and threw his luggage into the back seat of his car, he took one final look at his side yard and the small, dirty beach that looked almost clean in the midmorning sun. For a moment, he wished he hadn't done it. But he had done it, that was all there was to it. As he got into the car and started it, his mind seemed to be working at only about a thirty-percent capacity. He was now totally focused on the mechanics of driving the car down the driveway.

He had no idea where he was going. His plan was simply to head west. On the other side of Philadelphia he got on to 1-76 heading west and very soon after that he made the decision to drive all night, to maybe not stop until he was west of the Mississippi. His mind made several attempts to call up things to worry about but he pushed them all away. His thoughts remained on the open road and the freedom ahead.

After another hour or two had passed he began to feel hungry, a good sign, and he took the first exit off the Pennsylvania Turnpike that clearly indicated food. He saw the tall yellow arches of McDonalds and immediately decided on two Big Macs, two fries, a strawberry milkshake, and a large DietCoke. The weather was beautiful. Sunny and about 65 degrees. As he sat there with both front windows rolled down he began to notice the colors of the leaves on the trees in front of him on a hilly embankment that ran up along the side of the parking lot. They were just beginning to turn a bright red and yellow. He smiled to himself and started to daydream.

He remembered back to his childhood, to when he had been a Boy Scout and gone on his first overnight camping trip. It had been in the early fall. He had been so excited about it the night before he had barely been able to sleep and he remembered that he had been one of the first boys to fall asleep that night out in the woods. While the other boys sat around the campfire with the scoutmaster telling ghost stories, Cecil had fallen asleep in his sleeping bag under the stars.

He had been the first one up the next morning. He had climbed out of his bag, wet from sweating, and walked to the top of a small embankment similar to the one now in front of him. He had pissed, long and thoughtfully, into a small hole in the ground that surely must have been the home of a fox, a rabbit, or a snake. And while he was relieving himself he had noticed the colors of the leaves were just beginning to change to a bright red and yellow.

His daydream reminded his kidneys that he had to pee. He looked around the parking lot carefully, saw no one paying any attention to him, opened the car door, and very quickly ran up the embankment. Once up the hill he found the spot he was looking for.

After relieving himself and quickly devouring his meal, he was back on the road again and thinking about Fratino. He hadn't told Louis he was leaving town. He had warned him to lay low for a while, knowing it would make no difference yet feeling compelled to give some kind of warning. He had not told anybody he was leaving. Nobody knew where he was and that thought was exhilarating to him as he gently felt the layer of bills in the right side pocket of his trousers. He looked over into the passenger's seat and felt even more comfortable from the sight of the bulge in his madras jacket that lay across the seat. He was contemplating a brand new life. Why should he tell anyone where he was? Without the mistakes from his past he still might make himself a nice new life. He felt better than he had felt all day.

After driving for several hours, passing through some familiar parts of Ohio for what he knew might be the last time and fighting the compulsion to stop in Cleveland to say hello to his mother and father, he pulled into a truck stop. He ordered a huge plate of pancakes, sausage, and syrup for dinner. After a second cup of coffee while staring intensely at a Rand McNally map book he had just purchased, he went into the restroom to wash his hands and face. As he dried himself with a handful of brown, smelly, paper towels, his glasses and mapbook perched carefully on the sink next to him, a wave of fear fell over him as he heard his name being called. Fumbling quickly for his glasses and dropping the mapbook to the dirty, tile floor, he looked up at two truckers who had just walked into the restroom. One of them apparently shared his name.

After a moment of simply standing there in front of the long row of sinks, stunned, he reached down and picked up the map book, wiped it off with the damp brown towels he still held in his hand, and headed for the door. He walked quickly through the restaurant and out to his car. He drove thoughtfully, carefully, as though he were being followed by a police car. Soon, he began to relax again.

As evening fell over the highway and the sky grew dark, the headlights of the approaching cars became less glaring on his eyes. Cecil's thoughts drifted to sex. He began to feel himself pressing into the tightness of his pants. He imagined pulling into a motel, entering his room, and finding one of the hotel maids lying across the bed: naked, blond, heavy, and big breasted. She was pleasuring herself as she looked up at him, her eyes begging for him to take her. He grew more aroused and reached down to rearrange himself. He forced himself to start thinking about a destination and his new life ahead to take his mind off the maid.

He would have to find a small town somewhere and sell his car, buy another car, and move on to another small town and try to settle down. He thought of Arizona, New Mexico, and Wyoming. All exotic sounding places he had never seen. They sounded like good places to get lost and start over. Perhaps he could get a job selling shoes somewhere! Become part of the community.

Remarry. Have children. Start a brand new family. Who would ever know?

He thought of his father and knew he couldn't go home to visit for a long time. Kepler would be looking in Cleveland. Cecil would have to call his parents from wherever he settled down. He would tell them he was fine and that after some time had passed he would come to visit them. Even better, they could come and visit him. In his new home. They could be a part of his new life! He might have to move them of course. And would they want to leave Cleveland? Probably not. Oh well, he thought to himself, he would just have to figure out a way of seeing them.

He finally began to relax. He stopped changing the station on the radio so often and had stopped counting all red cars, a habit from childhood. He began to appreciate the rhythm of the road, the quiet slapping of the tires against the pavement and the gentle blowing of the wind through the two open side vent windows. The radio station he finally decided on was a classical station in Chicago and as he got closer the signal became stronger and the music more clear and free of static. He was unfamiliar with the station and although he knew the piece by Vivaldi they were playing, he wished he might soon hear the strains of some Verdi.

He noticed the fluorescent neon of a hotel sign shortly beyond the next exit ramp. He quickly made the decision to change lanes and take the exit. As he pulled into the parking lot of the motel he noticed its green vacancy sign was shining, almost glowing, near the door. He walked into the office to inquire about a room.

He was greeted by a short, fat woman in her late-thirties who wore a purple flowered dress. Her breasts bulged threateningly out from her chest as she asked Cecil if he was alone. Her face was worn and tired looking and her blond curly hair had fallen victim to too many cheap perms over the years. Her breasts were huge and Cecil felt himself growing again as he stood across from her on one side of the check-in counter.

He told her he needed a room for the night, although his eyes were trying to say something else; he was searching her face for a sign and expected to find it. She looked at him cautiously, glanced up at the clock on the wall, then back to him. As she walked over towards the front door, still examining him and noticing now the protrusion from below his belt, her own face began to grow warm. She locked the door and flipped the blue and white cardboard clock hanging there around to show she was closed. She turned back to him and asked if he would like to see where she lived to get an idea of what the rooms were like. He moved towards her quickly, drawn to her, following her down a short corridor to the front door of her small apartment.

Once inside, his hands reached out for the buttons of her purple flowered dress. As he unfastened her bra he felt her own chubby hands frantically beginning to unbuckle his pants. As they dropped to the floor along with his green boxer shorts she was upon him at once, down on her knees. He held himself together long enough to pull her back up against him before clumsily pushing her down on to the pink, quilted bedspread. As he fell on top of her fat layered body and felt himself sink deeply into her, the pleasure he felt as he suddenly let himself go was intense and he was suddenly very tired. As he rolled off of her on to his back and closed his eyes, he fell, almost immediately, into a deep sleep.

He awoke after about a half hour had passed and looked over at her. She was facing away from him, wearing only her bra and panties, and he felt a sudden revulsion from the thick rolls of fat which hung off of her body from her shoulders down to her knees. It was only when she turned around to face him that her breasts began to work on him again. He motioned her towards him and she moved quickly, unfastening her bra and letting it fall to the floor as she moved towards him. She was soon squatting over him, taking him up inside of her while her huge breasts hung menacingly over his face. And after they were done this time she tried to start a conversation with him.

"My, my, my how I've waited for you, Honeylamb. What is your name?" She was sitting next to him now on the edge of the bed running her short, thick fingers through her curly, sweaty mat of hair.

"Cecil," he responded.

"Cecil? Cecil who?"

He thought for a moment before replying, knowing he needed to come up with an Italian name, and when it came out he was pleased with how it sounded. "Cecil Martino."

"I'm Fanny, Cecil Martino, and the pleasure was all mine." She turned to face him, adding, "Where have you been all my life, Honeylamb?" She smiled what many years ago must have been a cute, even sexy, smile.

But to Cecil it was revolting. Her smile made her look almost like a cartoon character. "So," he began, "where exactly are we. When I pulled off the highway I wasn't paying a whole lot of attention."

"Not to directions I'd say, but to a certain other thing I would say!" She was fastening her bra in the back, her heavy arms bent awkwardly over her shoulders as she did so.

"Fanny. What kind of a name is that?" He was trying to be polite while inwardly he thought only of fleeing.

"Fanny? Oh that's just a nickname people gave me a long time ago. It kinda stuck. Real name is Frances. Frances Meriwether. Comin' up folks called me Franny and later on it changed to Fanny. And as to where you are, you're in Bristol, Indiana, right smat dab where you're supposed to be. Where you headed, Honeylamb?"

Cecil said nothing for a moment. "Bristol, Indiana" he thought to himself. "West!" he answered.

"West to where?" Fanny asked, stroking her hair and smiling.

"Not sure," Cecil answered.

"Why, I do believe my right nipple feels like you just about bit it off." She was speaking as though she were talking to herself while she gently massaged her right breast, staring down at it before looking back up at him. "But it would have been worth it, Honeylamb, worth every bit of it. You gettin' hungry?" She stood up to put on her clothes.

"As a matter of fact, I am hungry," he answered as he also began to get dressed. "What's on the menu, Fanny?" He was still thinking of leaving but he was truly hungry and knew how difficult it might be to find a place this late on a Sunday night.

"How about," she began, walking through a door that led to a small kitchen, "how about some red meat?" She turned to face him again. "Red meat for my wild animal?" She laughed a hideous laugh.

"Steak sounds good." He followed her into the kitchen and together they both stood staring at a frozen T-bone steak she had pulled from the freezer

"I think I still have some…" she said, now stooping down to look into the refrigerator, "yea, I still got 'em. Zuchini!" She pulled out a large green squash. "You like Zuchini, don't you? Why of course you do!" she said as she stood up. "Now you just sit down in there and make yourself comfortable while I cook everything right up."

"But the steak is still frozen!" Cecil complained, whining, "It'll be tough."

"You just go set yourself down and leave everything to me." She was gently guiding him back towards the bedroom.

As he sat in an armchair watching the last half hour of a *Startrek* rerun, he heard the soft humming sound of a microwave oven from the kitchen and began to feel a lot better about the meal.

They ate in bed. Afterwards, Fanny began to rub her right breast again, then both of them together. And once again, even tightly hidden behind the purple flowered dress, they began to work their magic on Cecil. But before he was again completely overwhelmed he motioned for her to stop. "No more, not now." He stood up and walked towards the bathroom. "Be right back."

Once inside the small tiled bathroom that smelled like a nail salon, he stared at himself in the mirror. He began to feel tired, very tired. Too tired to drive yet not sure if he wanted to stay. He washed his face and combed his black, wavy hair with one of Fanny's combs. As he set the comb down and applied a small strip of Pepsodent toothpaste to his right index finger and began cleaning his teeth, he decided to leave at once.

Walking back into the bedroom, the expression on Fanny's face made it clear that she knew he was leaving. Her sadness was evident in her soft, breaking voice. "You might come back again sometime? To see me?" Her eyes were filling with tears but she wasn't crying yet.

"Sure, Fanny. I will come back to see you. You can bet on it. Listen," he moved towards her front door, saying, "I'll send you a postcard from Wyoming." He left her front door open and walked towards the motel entrance. Once there he reached up to turn the blue and white cardboard clock sign back around again to where it read OPEN - PLEASE COME IN.

"Cecil?" She was now standing in the corridor near the front desk. She was crying, softly.

He walked over to her and kissed her on the forehead. "I'll come back and see you sometime. I promise." He turned to leave. At the door, he turned back to her with a smile and she returned it through her tears.

In his car, sitting in the parking lot before he pulled away, he watched the green fluorescent vacancy sign come back on again. He hadn't noticed her ever turning it off. A light rain was falling and as he turned the car around in the parking lot he glanced back at the front office. He saw Fanny standing behind the glass of the front door, waving goodbye.

As he pulled out on to the side road which led back up to the entrance ramp, he saw a sign for Bristol with an arrow pointing to the right. He decided to take a quick look at the town, thinking that perhaps he might even find another motel where he could get some sleep before morning. The road was a winding road, unusual for the generally flat terrain, and after driving for about a mile he saw a silhouette of the town ahead of him.

There were few lights on as he crossed the city limits sign and he saw no sign of a motel. Farther down the main road he noticed a sign over a tan colored building that said Ray's Oldsmobile. On the lot out in front of the building he saw a rather substantial selection of cars and RVs for sale, both new and used, and he decided that the following day he would be driving one of them. For now, he pulled his car into the parking lot in front of the dealership and parked. He turned off the lights, then the engine, put his seat all the way back, and within a few minutes he was sound asleep.

The next morning he was behind the wheel of a 21-ft. recreational vehicle, a 1975 Winnebago Chieftain. It was beige with blue and orange horizontal stripes. Inside, it was equipped with a bunk bed, a toilet and shower, a small refrigerator, a gas stove, and a small black and white TV.

As he turned on to the I-57 South freeway entrance he was smiling, proud of his purchase. He would save money on motels. He could shower when he wanted to. He

could cook when he wanted to. And no one would ever
begin to look for him in an RV! He could pass through
towns safely. Even if Kepler had people out looking for
him, no one would find him. He had traded in his car and
paid an extra three thousand dollars for it but he felt good
about it. It was worth it. As he drove down the highway
at a peaceful 55 mph in the right hand lane, he began to
think of the market.

It was Monday morning and he had to call his broker to close out his futures account. He would have the
balance bank-wired to the next major city, probably St.
Louis. He would have, after liquidating his position in
Swiss Francs and Soybeans, about thirty thousand dollars to work with. Not bad, he thought to himself, still
smiling.

He stopped at a Texaco station at a rest stop to make
the necessary phone calls. First, he needed to find a bank
in St. Louis. He got a listing of a bank from directory assistance by asking for the number of St. Louis National,
guessing at a name. They had come back with St. Louis
Federal and he decided that they would be as good as
any. After all, it was a simple transaction. They would
receive the funds from a Chicago bank and turn them
over to him.

He got an officer on the line and explained the situation. He told him he was moving to St. Louis and was
having the money wired into a new account. He assured
the banker that he would personally come into the bank
as soon as he got into town to sign the necessary papers
to open the account. For now, he asked if they would
simply receive the funds from the transferring bank in

Chicago. They told him they couldn't handle it that way. He would first have to come into the bank and open an account. Cecil got angry and hung up.

He tried a few more banks, guessing at names with directory assistance until he got the numbers. They all told him the same thing. They could do nothing without him first coming into the bank.

Very angry now, he hung up on the last banker and climbed back into the RV. He had forgotten to call his broker. Oh well, it could wait, he thought to himself. It would have to wait until he had a place to send the money. He started to drive away when the thought struck him that Clayton Brokerage Company was headquartered in St. Louis. He could have the funds transferred to a new account with them and then go by and pick up the check. He got back out of the RV and placed a call to his Chicago broker to order the liquidation and transfer.

The market was being good to him today, he was told by his broker. Why was he transferring his account to Clayton? "Is there a problem? Is there anything I can do to make you leave your account with us, Mr. Clemenzi?"

"No. Just do what I say and transfer the money. Close me out and send the balance to Clayton in St. Louis."

"But I need an account number," his broker explained.

Terribly frustrated, Cecil responded, "Just close me out, at the market. I'll call you back later." He hung up the phone. Back on the highway again, he began to cool down. He would take care of things when he got there. There should be no problem. Clayton would gladly accept the transfer thinking that they had a new client. They would also then have to release the funds to him on demand. For now, he thought to himself as he looked out the big front window at the Illinois farmland that stretched for miles around him, for now he would simply enjoy the scenery.

Later that afternoon, he saw the St. Louis Arch in the distance and as it grew closer his stomach began to control every thought. He knew he ought to eat before he called on Clayton Brokerage and as he took the Kingshighway exit, he soon found himself in a fashionable district of St. Louis known as the Central West End.

Barnes Hospital loomed over the entire area, its stark concrete structure in sharp contrast to the quaint, bouncy streets of red brick which led him onto Euclid Avenue. He saw restaurants on every corner and went into a state of mild panic as he looked for a place to park the RV. A public parking sign a half block off of Euclid caught his eye and he was parked within a few minutes.

He walked up Euclid, starving yet too curious to enter the first place he saw. He eventually ended up at an outdoor cafe called the Flamingo Cafe. The menu featured a wide variety of light items, sandwiches, and several Italian dishes. He ordered linguini with clam sauce, a Caesar salad, and a DietCoke.

After eating, he got directions from the waitress to Clayton, a small community a few miles west of downtown that was now the financial center of St. Louis. All of the major brokerage offices were located there, having moved from their downtown locations over the last few years due to urban blight and a great reluctance on the part of county residents to drive all the way downtown to make their investment decisions.

Once in Clayton he had a terrible time finding a parking place for the RV. The beautiful tree-lined streets were overflowing with parking meters and all of the meters were full. On the outskirts of Clayton he parked in a department store parking lot and walked several blocks back into the financial district to the offices of Clayton Brokerage Company. He was in a rather sour mood as he entered the lobby of this small, yet respected, commodity brokerage firm.

He was greeted by an attractive young black woman in her early twenties with straight red hair that had been gently curled so that it bounced just above her shoulders. She was the receptionist and she quickly introduced him to a broker halfway down an open corridor of partitioned offices. The broker's name was Bill Day. His Texas accent appeared to startle everyone seated near him almost as much as it did Cecil.

"So, Mr. Clemenzi. You watchin' those beans?" Bill Day's tall, gaunt appearance did not match his confident sounding drawl at all as he motioned for Cecil to sit down.

"What about the beans?" Cecil sounded antagonistic.

"Hell, they're up 22 cents!" Bill Day was elated. "You long?"

"Got out this morning. Listen, I'm here to open an account. I'm having my funds wired in from Chicago and I need an account number for the transfer. Can you do that?"

"Yes siree, right here. Let me just get the paperwork." With his eyes still on the quote machine he shouted for his assistant, "Shari, bring me up here a set of new account papers please. For Mr. Clemenzi." He then turned to face Cecil. "We'll get you set up here in no time."

After filling out the forms, Cecil walked over to a waiting area near the front of the office away from Bill Day. He sat down on a small couch and began to nervously rifle through a back issue of *FUTURES* magazine. He was soon interrupted by a tall, immaculately dressed man in his late thirties who introduced himself as Mark Barnett, the branch manager. He welcomed Cecil to St. Louis and tried to engage him in conversation.

"So, Mr. Clemenzi, You're from Chicago? I understand you are moving to St. Louis?"

"My accounts are in Chicago. Yes, I am thinking of moving here." Cecil tried to sound nonchalant, "Nice office."

Mr. Barnett smiled in appreciation and held out his hand again. "Again, welcome. Please don't hesitate to call me if I can be of any assistance to you." He moved away from Cecil towards the corridor of brokers.

Although it had been a harmless encounter, Cecil's nerves were shot. He asked the receptionist how long it might be and she called upstairs to New Accounts to find out.

"Your account is all set up, Mr. Clemenzi," she said as she hung up the phone. "Would you like to see Mr. Day again?"

"No, not really. Tell him I'll call him later. Have you got an account number there for me?" He had seen her writing down a number while on the phone.

"Right here." She handed him a piece of paper with the number written on it in neatly formed numerals. "Have a nice day, now."

"You too." He was turning to leave when he heard a shout from the general vicinity of Bill Day's office.

"Good Lord, look at those beans. They just took limit up!" Bill Day was excited.

Cecil turned to leave, shaking his head in dismay, remembering a time long ago when he had worked the pit, the dramatic rush of feelings that would so suddenly overcome all sensibility when prices moved quickly.

The next morning he called Bill Day from his hotel room at The Clayton Inn. He had decided against sleeping in the RV. A nice room with a bath, room service and cable TV had made him feel great and he was in a much better mood today.

Bill Day told him that the money was in the account if he was ready to put on a trade. Cecil thanked him, hung up, and redialed the same number, asking for the cashier. He gave her his name and account number and she said she would have the check ready for him by noon.

The check was drawn on a The First National Bank of Clayton and their main branch was right next door to Clayton Brokerage Company. By one o'clock Cecil was back on the road again. The president of the bank had not approved of him carrying thirty one thousand dollar bills on his person, but after a creative tale about how he only planned on using it to get a better deal on a new BMW he was buying that afternoon, the banker wished him good luck, marveling at the luxury of being able to spend $30,000 on a new 320i. That he had won it all in the soybean market seemed even more astounding to the banker than the purchase of the car. The fact that he had made up the whole story, quickly, and in desperation to get the cash, pleased Cecil even more than the story had the banker. As he drove west on Highway 40, leaving St. Louis behind, he laughed out loud at his own cleverness. His right hand tapped nervously on his pants pocket where the bills were neatly folded and secure, and looked out the big front window at the wide open spaces in front of him.

Late that night he pulled into a roadside campground just over the Kansas border in Colorado. He hooked up the water and electricity to the RV, cooked a pound of hamburger on his gas stove, showered, and fell asleep. The next morning he woke up early and was back on the road by seven. He decided to stop somewhere for breakfast and he took an exit that led him into a small town called Flagler. He found a coffee shop in a small shopping strip, parked, and went inside.

The place looked almost as it must have looked thirty years ago. Booths with large cushioned vinyl seats of faded maroon ran down the entire side of the room. The counter was thick, formica topped, and adorned with small round stools mounted on dull, chrome posts. Cecil sat down at a center booth and began to look at the menu.

As the waitress brought him a cup of coffee, he noticed another customer walk in and sit down in the booth in front of him. He was an older man, about seventy, and he looked like he was dying. His face was full of age and his eyes held no light at all as he ordered a plain English muffin and a DietCoke. As much as Cecil enjoyed drinking his DietCokes it struck him as odd that someone would order one so early in the morning. The more he looked at the man, the more convinced he became that he was dying. A slow death, perhaps cancer. This peculiar breakfast order was probably one of the few things he was allowed to eat.

He ate it without showing the slightest degree of enjoyment. He drank his soda the same way. Cecil looked around the diner and over to the counter where a group of construction workers were just finishing breakfast, probably big ones he thought: pancakes, eggs, bacon, sausage, and lots of coffee. They were standing up to leave and one of them in an old green and black flannel shirt shouted down to a homely looking waitress for her to "stay out of the bar rooms," laughed heartily, and walked out with his friends.

The old, dying man in front of him was also ready to leave as Cecil's own breakfast was served. The scrambled eggs looked fine, the bacon greasy, and his toast was covered with a thick layer of bright yellow margarine. Two small packets of apple jelly were perched on the side of the plate. Cecil ate the meal quickly, thinking mostly of how awful it was that the average American diet was so greasy.

As he stood to leave, after leaving a few dollars on the table to cover his check, he became acutely aware of just how greasy his own meal had been. As he walked out into the morning sun he belched loudly and felt a little better. He stood there staring at his Chieftain, not liking it nearly as much as he thought he would.

He still hadn't called his wife, Kathy. Perhaps he never would. Maybe she would just think he had been knocked off. She had plenty of money in the bank, and Louis and her mother would take good care of her. Well, at least her mother would be able to take care of her. Maybe it would be better if she thought he was dead. After all, if he were going to start all over again, why not start fresh? He felt good about everything, everything except the meal he had just eaten, and soon he was back on the highway.

He sold the RV later that day at a dealership in Cheyenne, Wyoming. He lost some money on the deal but he didn't really care. He took a room for the night at a small hotel down the street from the dealership.

The Rand McNally map book, his two blue suitcases, his gun, and his money were his only possessions now. After spending the night in Cheyenne, he took a bus the next morning into Laramie, the place he had decided to call home for a while. The Realtor was friendly enough, though Cecil had been expecting someone a little more 'cowboyish' looking, and a small brick house for rent a block off of Grand Avenue soon became the new home of Cecil Martino, a poor man who had just recently lost his wife and children in an automobile accident back in Coral Gables, Florida. He had moved to these new environs, as they called it out here, to ease the pain and forget the sorrow.

Cecil's first few days in his new house were full of excitement. The small red, brick home, which had come furnished, had two bedrooms, one bath, a living room that adjoined a small dining room, and a modest sized kitchen. The neighborhood he was in was about twenty five years old and the trees were of good height, unlike some of the newer neighborhoods in Laramie. His front yard had a manicured look to it and he was thrilled to find that an old man named Horace would keep it looking that way for an extra $40 a month. The Realtor had told him that Horace had kept up yards in the neighborhood for a long time and could be trusted to do a good job. Cecil's first few days were devoted more towards enjoying the newness of his surroundings than worrying about the past.

The first neighbor he met was Laura Frost. She was in her mid-thirties, divorced, extremely attractive, and had an eight-year-old daughter named Tanya. Laura had moved to Laramie with her husband five years ago. He worked for a consulting firm and as soon as they were settled in he was assigned to a temporary position overseas. Scarcely another six months had passed before she received a letter from him wishing her the best and saying he was very sorry it had to end this way. She had then taken it upon herself to get a job at the telephone company and stick it out here with her daughter in their new home.

Cecil first met Laura the day after he moved in. She was just coming home from work and he was standing in the driveway after having taken a short walk into town to buy a paper. It was about four-thirty in the afternoon and the wide blue Wyoming sky was cloudless. The weather was starting to get cool. Cecil had been staring up at the sky when Laura honked the horn of her Mazda as she pulled into the driveway. She had waved to him after honking and when she got out of the car she walked around to the other side, near to where he was standing, and introduced herself.

"I'm Laura Frost, your neighbor. Welcome!" She had a southern accent that felt warm and seemed to invite a certain intimacy.

Cecil walked towards her and shook hands, "Hello Laura." Then, looking at her daughter, he added, "And who's this?"

"This is Tanya." The little girl mumbled, "Hi," looking away as she spoke.

"My name is Cecil. Cecil Martino. Just moved out here from Florida." The story telling was getting easier.

"Florida? Oh my! I grew up in South Carolina. I haven't seen Florida in years. We used to go down there on vacation, you know, to the beaches? God that trip in the car used to take forever. Whereabouts in Florida, Cecil?"

"Coral Gables."

"Oh, I've never been there. Guess Florida has really changed since I used to go there."

"It has grown." Cecil wanted to change the subject. Looking back up at the sky he said, "Sky sure seems big out here."

"Of course it does. That's why they call it Big Sky Country. Haven't you heard that expression yet?" She walked back to the trunk of her car and began to unload the groceries. "Here Tanya, you take this one, hon."

Cecil said, "Nice to meet you." He walked backwards towards his own driveway.

"Nice to meet you too, Cecil." Laura smiled at him as she shut the trunk. Adjusting the grocery bags in her arms, she began walking up her driveway. "We'll be seeing you now."

Cecil waved goodbye and walked back up towards his house. Once inside, he walked back into his bedroom and stared at himself in the mirror. His green golf slacks and yellow alligator shirt needed pressing and his face looked like he had just come out of a deep sleep. He was upset for not taking better care of himself.

He walked out to the phone in the hall, picked up the small purple and brown colored telephone directory and began to look up laundries. He found only one that delivered and when he called them he was told they would be closing at six. He made arrangements for them to pick up his clothes the next morning and he was assured that he would have them back late the following Monday. He then decided that tonight he would go shopping for new clothes as he caressed the roll of thousand dollar bills in his pocket.

He opened up the Laramie Lance, the local paper, and began to glance through it for a men's clothing store advertisement. He walked into the dining room and turned on the overhead light, a cheap chandelier that hung slightly askew above a small rectangular dining table. He saw an advertisement for a western store on Third Street and saw they were open until nine. He called the number of a store listed in the ad from his kitchen phone to get directions. The store was only about a half a mile west of him and straight out Grand. He thought about calling a cab but decided to walk.

After shaving, washing his face, and combing his thick oily hair that badly needed trimming, he walked out the door. Grand Avenue was only a short distance up his own street and west was to the left. In ten minutes he could see the store. He enjoyed walking, always had, and it was only after the third car of locals gave him a strange glance as they drove past him that he realized his green pants and yellow shirt were not traditional garb for the streets of Laramie. For a split second he recalled his Catholic schoolboy's uniform. But, he encouraged himself, after tonight, after he bought some western duds, he'd fit right in!

Cecil tried on various outfits and liked nearly everything that was suggested to him by the clerk. Within an hour he was weighted down with bags and packages. Leaving the store, both hands full, he realized how difficult it might be to walk back home carrying everything. He decided to take the bus on Grand Avenue. He stood at the bus stop for over fifteen minutes and finally the bus arrived. He was smiling, enjoying himself immensely, as he paid the fare and found a seat.

The trip down Grand only took about three or four minutes. He got off the bus only a block from his street. As he was walking towards home, burdened with his packages, he heard a familiar honking sound. It was Laura again. She pulled up along beside him, rolled down the window on the passenger side, and shouted, "Thought that was you. Looks like you've got your hands full?"

Cecil nervously bent down to see her more clearly through the window. "Hello Laura."

"Been shopping, have we?"

Examining his packages, he nodded in the affirmative. "Guess I over did it a little."

"Hop in," she offered politely.

After putting his packages in the back seat, he got in the car and said, "I really appreciate this."

"What are neighbors for?" She responded.

"Where's Tanya?"

"She's at home," Laura answered.

"By herself?" Cecil affected alarm.

"Oh she's fine. I just ran up to the store to get some ice cream. She's watching *Family Ties*. Didn't want to miss anything, you know?" Laura seemed to be an extremely happy person. As she pulled the car into the driveway she invited him in. "You want to join us for some dessert? After you put your stuff away?" She looked into the back seat. "What all did you buy anyway?" She sounded excited, as though she truly wanted to see.

"New clothes," Cecil answered, looking down at his wrinkled green slacks. "Gotta fit in out here, you know."

"I've got a wonderful idea. Why don't you bring in your packages and you can model your new clothes for me and Tanya."

Cecil declined immediately. "No, I don't think so." Then he asked her, "What flavor ice cream?" He was smiling.

"Two flavors. Cherry Vanilla, that's for me, and a half gallon of Rocky Road."

"I love Rocky Road." He opened the car door. "I'll be over after I take this stuff inside, all right?"

"See you shortly," Laura replied as she got out on her side and walked towards her front door.

Later, after they had all eaten ice cream and Tanya had been sent to bed, and Cecil had explained his tragic Florida story to her, Laura suggested that they have a drink. Cecil agreed to an Amaretto on the rocks. Noticing that *Hill Street Blues* was just coming on TV, he commented to her, "You're sure you don't want me to take off?"

"You just sit right there Cecil Martino. You're not leaving until you hear my latest poem!" Her energy level seemed to increase as the evening wore on.

"Poem?" Cecil looked at her stupidly.

"That's right. Your new neighbor is a poet. Didn't know that did you. Not yet published but a poet none the less. Now you just sit there and listen."

She opened up a blue spiral notebook she had been holding, walked over and turned the sound down on the TV, stood in front of the screen so that the picture was still partly visible between her legs, and began to recite her poem.

> Throbbing, his member rose, surging and hot
> Involving, her insides were tied in a knot
> Feeling, a softness of skin touching skin
> Entry, a hardness so smooth moving in

After hearing the first line Cecil had fixed his gaze on the activities of Captain Frank Furillo engaged in a heated conversation with Joyce Davenport on the television screen between Laura's legs. Realizing she had just completed the first poem, or the first stanza, whatever it was, Cecil felt obligated to look up at her, and he did.

"Erotic," she announced casually before continuing. "You know, like Erotic Art?" Her southern accent grew heavier with the next line.

> A friction, machine-like, you move in and out
> Addiction, warm wrapping of legs all about

Cecil stood up. "I'm sorry Laura, but are you sure you want to read this stuff to me? I mean …" He looked back towards the bedroom to indicate his concern for Tanya. "Are you sure she's asleep? What if she is listening?"

Laura's face looked hurt. "You don't like it." She pouted.

"I do like it. Really, I do. It's just that, well, we don't even really know each other."

"Why, of course we do. You live over there and I live over here. We're neighbors." For the first time Cecil noticed a strange look in her eyes, a twisted creepy kind of look he hadn't noticed before, and after appearing for only a moment it was gone again, replaced by Laura's warm, friendly smile from earlier.

"Well, I guess I just feel a little uncomfortable, that's all." Cecil looked directly at her as he spoke. In his look he tried to convey that he was ready to forget the whole thing and sit back down. Or even leave. Whatever she thought best.

"Now, now," Laura comforted him. "You just sit there and listen. I'm almost through it anyway."

Conditioned we move in warm lubrication
Affliction a sexual communication

"Well," she added, "What do you think? I call it *Sexual Communication.*"

"It's nice. Really, it is." Cecil began to feel the first initial signs of an erection as he watched Joyce Davenport gaze longingly at Captain Furillo on the TV screen behind Laura.

After a second poem, Laura suggested another drink. As she walked into the kitchen to make the drinks, Cecil knew he should probably tell her he had to leave. But he didn't. They finished their drinks and watched the rest of *Hill Street Blues* in silence. When it was over, Cecil stood up, thanked her for a wonderful evening, complimented her on the poetry again, and said goodbye.

Cecil barely slept that night, tossing and turning and having what could only be described as sexual nightmares about Laura. He awoke the next morning to the sound of a lawn mower. Looking outside he saw Horace mowing Laura's yard. He closed his window, which he had left cracked all night. As he did he looked directly across at Laura's house. He rubbed his eyes to make sure he really saw her doing what she was doing. From his window he could look directly into her bathroom window, where she was standing there naked, her breasts totally exposed to him, and she was waving at him good naturedly. He waved back to her and quickly climbed back into his bed.

After trying to sleep some more he finally gave it up. He got out of bed, showered, put on one of his new outfits, and went out for breakfast. He spent the day walking around town, poking into out of the way shops and taverns, just to get some kind of feel for the place. Late in the afternoon, after eating an early dinner, he took in a movie at the Main Street Cinema, purposely putting off going home for as long as possible.

He got home at ten o'clock. He saw Laura's car parked in her driveway, noticed the dim light from her TV, and quietly went inside his own house. He turned on only one small light in the hall on his way to his bedroom. He fell asleep quickly and slept soundly.

The next morning he awoke to the sound of Laura knocking on his front door. She wanted to invite him to accompany her and Tanya on a day trip to a state park. He politely declined. As he shut the door, he was relieved that he would have the day to himself.

He began by going out and buying a new car. Actually, a 1981 Jeep Cherokee. He figured it would be the right kind of car to own out here, just in case he wanted to do some exploring. And that's exactly what he decided to do after leaving the dealership. As he drove west on the main highway just outside of Laramie, he began to feel a cold, clammy sense of dread, a panicky feeling, as though he were afraid of something and didn't know what it was. He cut short his drive and returned home at once.

That night, the weird feelings still lingered. When Laura dropped by at nine thirty, after putting her "very tired little girl to bed after a big day at the lake," Cecil began to feel even more panicky than he had before. That crazy look was in Laura's eyes again and he was only halfway aware of the conversation. She was telling him all about their day, showing him her sunburn on her chest and thighs, and rambling on and on about some kind of fish she had caught that day. Cecil sat down at his dining room table and buried his face in his hands, finally getting her attention.

"Are you all right? Are you sick? Cecil, what's wrong?" She moved closer to him and felt his forehead. "You feel hot."

He snapped at her, saying, "I feel clammy and cold and my head hurts."

"Oh dear. We better get you into bed. Here, come along now with me."

"I'll be all right," he protested.

"Don't you dare argue with me, you poor thing. Stand up now and follow me. I'm gonna get you into bed. She began leading him into the bedroom. "After all you've been through, all the grief and all, it's no wonder you're sick. And the fever! I just know you're running a high fever. I am a mother you know."

"Please," Cecil said to her, "I'll be all right." They had just reached his bed and he sort of fell into it.

"Oh dear," Laura was sounding more and more concerned, "How do you really feel? Cecil, do you think I should call a doctor? Or 911? I think I better. You look terrible. You just lie down here and rest." She moved out of the room before he could gather the strength to stop her.

"No need," he began to say, before slipping into a kind of delirium. He opened his eyes and saw her when she walked back into the room again. He thought he saw her taking her top off and waving to him. Then he was sure she hadn't. She was still standing right by his bed, still wearing her top. Then he blacked out.

He came to as he heard the doctor talking to Laura, saying there was no need for the hospital. Something about his "good vitals." He also heard Laura telling the doctor she could take real good care of him, that he had just lost his entire family, and that he was brand new to the area. He was from Florida. Then he blacked out again.

In a dream he saw a ship moving through the water and the sky was dark purple, almost green in places, and he saw Kevin Kepler at the helm, wearing a Captain's cap and smiling. Then he saw Kevin standing across from him in the trading pit, smiling the same smile. His face was partially blocked out by the frantic waving of trader's hands and small, square pastel sheets of paper. And there in the sea of hands, there was Laura, standing next to Kevin with her top off. She was waving her top in her hands through a flotilla of small pastel sails. The sails were attaching themselves to boats, and the boats were then surrounded by the waves, and the rough ocean water was pounding against the side of the big ship. Kevin was still at the helm and Laura was with him and her top was off.

"No!" His screaming woke him up as Laura was putting a damp wash cloth across his forehead. She was speaking to him in a soft comforting tone of voice, though he could not quite make out what she was saying. Just as he was about to pass out again he heard her clearly now. She was reciting one of her poems, her erotic poetry.

He woke up the next day and felt like he had been sleeping for days. Laura was no longer there. A note was taped to his chest on a 3-inch square pastel green piece of paper. It had her phone number on it and said she would be right back. As he lay there waiting for her to return, he fell asleep again.

She woke him up that night to give him some chicken bouillon she had made. He asked her what night it was. She told him it was Monday night. He felt like he had lost a day or two and was feeling that same cold, clammy feeling again.

The next day he felt a little better. He got out of bed, took a shower, and even took a short walk outside. He had insisted that Laura go to work and stop pampering him. The thought of calling his mother was overwhelming. Just to hear her voice. He couldn't have called her with Laura in the house. He needed some time alone just to figure out what he would say to her, how he would explain his disappearance. He would have to caution her that he was in trouble and was being sought by someone who would probably kill him if they found him. The more he thought about these things the worse he felt. He finally decided to just call her.

Cecil's mother was so happy to hear from him. She told him that his wife had called and left a message. That she understood and still loved him, that she was worried about him and knew it must have been something very serious for him to leave so suddenly. She had assumed he was in trouble and when certain people had come to the house looking for him, she had told them that she didn't know where he was or when he might return. His mother told him that he should call his wife and let her know he was okay, that it would be the right thing to do as a good husband. She told Cecil that his sister, Rebecca, was living in Annapolis and gave him the number. She told him to call his sister and to please take care of himself.

CHAPTER 7

Over a week had passed since Kevin's return from Bermuda and Virginia was still having problems with lightheadedness and disorientation. When he got back home she began to sense a distance between them, even though he still held her tightly when he hugged her. He seemed preoccupied, almost possessed about something, and she worried about him too much. He began to spend more time away from the ranch, and when he did come home he sat alone in his study as though waiting for something extremely important to happen.

She had seen Bill and Joe only once and that was the day after her father came home. They had flown in with *Ma Bell* and landed in the open meadow behind the house. She wasn't outside when it landed or she would have seen Bill and Joe removing a long, cigar-shaped object wrapped in canvas from the helicopter and carrying it into the barn before coming up to the house. Once inside, they spent most of their time in Kevin's study. They seemed different too, also preoccupied, less jovial than usual. Bill had spoken to her briefly before leaving, mostly small talk. That was a week ago and she hadn't seen them since.

She was now outside near the stables. It was a beautiful autumn afternoon and in the garden near the side of the house, huge orange pumpkins sat on the lawn surrounding the garden, just as they did every year before Halloween. They were the last item to be taken from the garden, except for a few radishes, and the potatoes of course. All of the other vegetables had been picked and eaten, or stored by Bertha.

When Virginia was small, the pumpkins had fascinated her more than any other part of the garden, how they started off as small yellow globes and quickly grew into majestic orange pumpkins. She had always enjoyed carrying the baby ones into the grassy area next to the garden where they would have plenty of room to grow. All around them the grass was cut short. Yet underneath them, when she moved the big ones just a little, long blades of grass would spring out in search of light and water. The sight of the big, orange pumpkins clinging to their vines for life gave her a feeling of hope that stayed with her for a few minutes before fading.

Her feelings of depression were getting worse, so bad that she had finally said something to Bertha about it, and Bertha went directly to Kevin about it. He had come to her and apologized for his distance, explaining to her that it was only temporary and would soon be over.

His decision to call Mike Chandler in Annapolis was made quickly. Perhaps in another time, a better time, he might not have called him. He might have tried to handle the situation himself. Kevin knew he was capable of taking care of his daughter, capable of making her feel good about life. But that was in ordinary times.

Today was the day that Mike was supposed to come down for his first consultation with Virginia and she was nervous. She was tired of taking Valiums and tired of feeling dizzy. She just wanted to get better. As she stood there looking at the pumpkins, she felt better than she had all day. She had awakened that morning feeling sad and had spent most of the morning trying to shake it by watching Bertha iron clothes in the den, like she had done as a little girl when she was upset. Bertha had suggested that she "take a little walk, get some air, stretch your legs, even go see how those pumpkins are doing."

Kevin was off riding one of his motorcycles. He had been riding his bikes a lot more lately. It had a soothing effect on him and helped him focus more clearly on what was going on around him and what he needed to do about it. When he had first found out about the attack on Mr. and Mrs. Hollingsworth, he spent most of his time just sitting and thinking, alone in his study. It had been Megan, trying to suggest something that might make him feel better, that might bring him out of his seemingly miserable state, who suggested that he go for a ride, and it had helped.

Now, as he sped down a long hilly stretch of road, he felt like it was all starting to come together. Bill had called that morning and told him about a lead he was following up on somewhere in Indiana, where he had found Cecil's car at a used car dealership. Kevin knew they would find him soon, he knew it was just a matter of time.

When he had first discovered Clemenzi was behind all of this, he had a difficult time believing it. His run-in with Clemenzi had been so long ago and so insignificant to Kevin. Commodity trading was full of risk, exorbitant risk. It always had been and anyone that played the game knew it. Clemenzi had understood the risk. Kevin figured that Cecil must have simply snapped and was operating on another level, a dangerous level, and was probably capable of doing just about anything. And this was why Kevin wanted to find him before anything else happened.

His thoughts began to center on Virginia. She was getting no better and he knew that none of Meg's former doctors would be any help. He knew his daughter well enough to know that she was reaching out for something and not getting it. His decision to call Mike Chandler had been the only sensible option. And when he had run the idea by her before calling him, the glimmer in her eyes had been enough to dispel any doubts.

As he flew down the highway now, approaching eighty miles per hour, he began to think about the day after his return and how he had handled the one punk Joe had thoughtfully and so correctly left alive. He had been young, about twenty-five, and when Kevin shot off his right ear as he began to question him the guy began to cry. Holding on to the bloody nub, which was all that was left of his ear, the guy told Kevin as much as he knew. He had been rather easy to break. He told Kevin about the guy that had hired him, a guy who ran a big party boat business over in Ocean City and was well connected, last name Fratino. It only took Kevin a few hours to make the necessary calls and discover that Fratino had a sister named Kathy, and that she was married to Cecil Clemenzi.

II

Mike was seated at his desk, waiting for his next patient, when he received the call from Kevin. The time that had passed since he last saw Kevin or Virginia seemed like months, though it had only been a couple of weeks. His feelings for Virginia had diminished somewhat but he still wanted to see her more than anything.

He had stopped seeing Marcia a week before. She had accepted it rather well, seeing it as only a phase of unrest in a relationship destined to go on forever. She had even been somewhat flippant about it, which had pissed him off. He had struggled for days to find a way of telling her it was over and when he finally told her she laughed at him.

He told Kevin he could be there at three o'clock. Kevin insisted on him spending the night, possibly even staying for a few days. It was a big house, he explained, plenty of room. Then he added, "We're all very grateful to you for saving her life, but I think she really needs some help now."

He left the office in a hurry, telling Nancy that an emergency had come up and he would be out of town for the next few days, possibly longer. He instructed her to cancel his appointments for the next week and refer all of his patients to Dr. Brown, another local psychologist he knew well, and to give no one his phone number where he could be reached in case of emergency, no one except Richard Cory. He felt comfortable with Cory knowing where he was. He knew he would have a lot of free time on his hands while staying at the ranch and Kevin would expect him to take a call from a patient every now and then.

He had come to think of Richard more as a friend than a patient. He had even met him once for breakfast at Chick & Ruth's and once for drinks at a pub on Dorchester. He was breaking the rules he learned in school about therapist/patient relations, but he really didn't care. He liked the guy. And Richard seemed to need a friend more than a therapist. Even though Richard did spend most of the time talking about unrequited love and out of body experiences, this was about the only thing that held Mike's interest anymore, except for thinking about Virginia.

He drove home for a shower and to pack some clothes. He hadn't been this excited since seventh grade, when he had fallen for Sally McDonald and somehow stolen her away from the jock she was going steady with for a weekend in Rehoboth! As he packed for his trip to see Virginia, he felt just as nervous as he had back then with Sally.

He tried to take his mind off of it by thinking about the out of body experiences Richard Cory had been telling him about. Richard believed he could, his soul that is, leave his physical body. He had told Mike of several startling occurrences through which he had proven it. He had been a guinea pig in a para-psychology study at the University of British Columbia in Vancouver back in the early seventies. He even brought Mike an armful of documentation and lab results showing how he had actually done it. And it all looked very official, signed by various physicians and professors.

He claimed he could leave his body in one place, travel for miles, and then come back again hours later. The one danger here was that some other soul, perhaps even an evil one, might take over his body while he was out of it and leave him out there all alone in search of a new home. At first, it had sounded so far fetched. But after a small demonstration one afternoon in Mike's office, when Richard put himself in a trance for a few minutes, he came out of it telling Mike what he would see if he rushed down to the corner market. Who he would see inside, what they would look like, what they would be wearing, what they would be buying. Reluctantly, Mike walked down to the corner store and found it to be very close to what Richard had described.

To Richard Cory it didn't seem like such a big deal, these OBE's. In fact, he preferred to spend more time talking about his bad luck with love. He said love was just a matter of some great destiny, some grand design that no one had any control over. Love would simply occur when it was meant to be and that was that. Unfortunately, for Richard Cory, this had simply not happened often enough.

The trip to the ranch in Virginia was about 130 miles. It was noon when he began and he knew, after stopping for lunch, he would arrive at three. The day was chilly though it felt like it might get warmer. The blue sky was covered with thick cumulous clouds and as the sun moved behind them it suddenly felt cooler again.

As Mike got close to where the ranch was located, he looked at the notes he had taken from Kevin on the phone, just to make sure he was going the right way. His mind, though he tried to slow it down, was racing. He knew he had to calm down and present a somber, professional composure when he got there. Thinking about how difficult that could be made him feel even more nervous. He reached into the glove box and pulled out a small prescription bottle of Serax, a tranquilizer he took on rare occasions. He took one of them. The small pink and white capsule got stuck in his throat before he managed to produce enough saliva to wash it down the rest of the way. He pulled into a Shell station and bought a Coke to wash the pill down completely.

The station was on a rural highway. He didn't know it at the time but the loud roar of a motorcycle, traveling very fast as it sped past the station, was Kevin Kepler, on his way home from a ride. Mike hung around the station making small talk with the attendant about the weather and tobacco and whether or not smoking really caused cancer. After a short while he felt the Serax start to mellow him out. He said goodbye to the friendly gas station attendant, confirming with him that his directions were right, and he was off.

He slowed down as he approached the main gate of the ranch. His first impression was that it was not as large of a place as he had expected. He saw the stables, the barn, and the old red tractor. He saw the orange pumpkins too, even though from such a distance they were very small. The house was not as big as he had imagined. It was a beautiful colonial style frame house with blue shingles and the customary verandah that surrounded and almost seemed to support the structure of the house itself. The driveway was paved and the grass along the edge of it had been recently mowed and edged. As he slowly drove towards the house, the smells of the stables became slightly noticeable and then they were gone, replaced by the smell of fresh air that hung to the light gentle breeze above the MG's open roof. He parked the car in an area off to the side of the driveway that appeared to be a designated parking area and paused for a minute staring at his small leather suitcase in the back seat. Should he take it in with him now? Or come back for it? He decided to leave it. He walked up to the front porch and before he was halfway up the gray steps he heard the front door opening and felt, even before he saw her, Virginia's presence.

She was wearing a simple white silk blouse and tight designer jeans that had been washed a lot. This was the first time he had ever seen her hair the way it looked after a shampoo, conditioner, and a blow dry. It was an even more beautiful dark auburn color than it had been before. Her skin was still lovely though it too had changed color. It was noticeably pale. Her smile, both from her eyes as well as her mouth, however, had not changed at all. Seeing her again was an overwhelming experience for him, so much so that he stopped one step short of the porch just to look at her, to smile right back at her.

When he began to walk again he forgot about the last step. Though he didn't fall, he stumbled. Then he quickly regained his balance and let his eyes and his smile meet back up with hers.

"Hi," she said, passively, lacking her usual spunkiness.

"Good afternoon, young lady." As soon as he said it he felt stupid. He ignored this feeling and moved closer to her, just as Meg appeared in the doorway behind her.

"Good afternoon, Dr. Chandler." She was cheerful in greeting him. "Welcome to Virginia."

"Please, not doctor. Call me Mike. It's a pleasure to meet you Mrs. Kepler."

"Megan. Call me Meg." She held out her hand to shake hands. She seemed slightly uncomfortable in addressing him by his first name.

"Well," Mike looked back to Virginia, "not feeling so well?"

She smiled sheepishly, responding, "Not so good."

"Where can we go to talk?" He surprised himself at how cool he sounded; the pill was working. "Meg? Have you thought about where Virginia and I could talk?"

"Oh, goodness gracious. I'm so sorry. Please come in." She turned and scurried back inside still talking. "I'll show you to the study. It's right in here. I think I heard Kevin come in awhile ago. Let me see." Approaching the door to the study, she knocked softly before opening it. "Hon? Oh!" she sounded surprised, "Why, you're not even in here." She turned back to face Mike and saw Kevin just entering through the front door.

"Looking for me?" He walked towards Mike. "Mike. Good to see you."

"Nice to see you, too," Mike responded.

"We were just discussing where your daughter and I might be able to have a chat?"

"Of course, well," he looked at Virginia. "Where do you want to have your first chat with Dr. Chandler, dear?" Kevin seemed pleased, even relieved, that Mike had come.

"Mike," interjected Mike, "please, everyone just call me Mike."

"Fine," Kevin said, pausing, looking up at Mike and perhaps showing the slightest bit of irritation before covering it with a smile, "Mike."

Virginia spoke up, "How about outside? Would that be okay?" She was asking Mike.

"Outside is fine," Mike said. "Front or back?"

"Out back. Here, follow me. See you guys later." She turned to leave the room, expecting Mike to follow.

He felt uncomfortable as he walked past Meg and Kevin, smiling and adding, "See you later," softly as he passed them. Once out the back door and down the steps, following Virginia, he was fine again. She stopped about fifty feet out from the house under an elm tree that had somehow survived a century or more without falling victim to disease, and sat down in the grass just within the shade of the tree. Mike caught up with her and sat down in the sunlight next to the shadow, only a few feet away from her yet far enough to look professional about it.

He asked her a few basic questions and she began talking about her thoughts and her life quite effortlessly. Fifteen minutes went by before he spoke again. She told him about the dizziness, how she had fainted, and how she had been taking Valiums for it. She then started talking about Nathan, about how she had never really felt like she loved him in a romantic way, that it had been more of a friendship. But now that he was gone she was crushed.

At this point Mike felt compelled to interrupt, wanting to ask if they had had a sexual relationship but instead saying, "That's all quite natural, Virginia. Really, it is. You lost someone very close to you and it hurts. Your emotions can get kind of backed up when you lose someone. All kinds of things run through your mind. What you could have said and didn't. What you could have done and didn't. You know," he paused, "grief can be overwhelming. And you're grieving the loss of someone who was very close." He paused again, as if preparing to ask an important question. "Did you ever, as a child, have a pet? A dog? Or a cat?"

She stared blankly back at him. "A horse." She paused before continuing. "I still have her." Her eyes lit up a little as she thought about her horse and she wanted to abruptly end the session and take Mike over to see her, yet she didn't move.

"Did you ever lose a pet?" Mike asked her, more solemn now.

She hesitated before answering. "Yea. Binkie. A small black and white spaniel my Mom and Dad gave me when I was five. He just disappeared one night, just like that. In the morning he was gone."

"How did you feel?" Mike asked her. "Did you think he had run away?"

"Or was stolen, I guess." Virginia stretched out in the shady grass and looked up into the branches of the elm. "I never did find out what happened to him."

"And yet," Mike continued, "I'm sure you wished you had been nicer to him while he was around? Fed him more treats? Played with him more often?"

"I was only six when he left," she sat up on her elbows and looked up at Mike quizzically. "I don't remember how I felt." She paused before asking, "What are you getting at?"

Mike had felt it coming before she asked and explained to her, "I was trying to show you how terrible a thing grief can be. And how your feelings about Nathan are absolutely normal, healthy feelings."

"Oh," she said.

Mike decided that enough had been said for now. Virginia seemed restless. She was trying to be polite about it but he could tell she was growing tired of his questions. "So? What do you think? Am I hired?" he asked her, trying to be humorous.

She looked directly at him. As the sun hit her hair and she smiled, the gleam from her eyes made him feel certain even before she spoke, "You're hired."

He almost reached out to put his hands on her shoulder but stopped himself, instead saying, "You're going to be just fine." He looked away from her, towards the stables, where he could hear the sounds of the horses and they sounded restless.

"Do you know what's going on with my father?" She completely altered the mood with her next question. "Do you know what he's planning to do?"

"What do you mean?" Mike felt sure, just for a second, that she meant her father was planning on doing something to him.

"To these men," she began to explain, "whoever it was that tried to kill me, and did kill Nathan, and then tried to kill Mr. and Mrs. Hollingsworth?"

"What?" Mike responded, stunned.

"You must promise me that you won't tell my father," she continued, as though she had prepared herself in advance for what she was about to say. "I overheard my father talking on the phone the other night. He's tracking down someone he feels is responsible for all of this. I know he has to stop them but I just don't want anything else to happen. Maybe, with you here, he likes you a lot you know, maybe with you here we could stop him from doing anything else about it. You know, we could just, well, you could talk to him, couldn't you? In a roundabout way, of course. Somehow maybe you could say something? I don't know." She held her head in her hands and stared over at the stables, saying, "The whole thing is making me crazy."

"What are you saying? You mean, the accident, the accident in the boat? I don't—" Mike paused as the story sunk in.

"Yea. That's right. One of my Dad's old enemies is out to settle a score."

"Jesus Christ!" Mike exclaimed. His new demeanor was one of protective concern as he continued, "Virginia, I'm going to have to talk to your father. He simply cannot put you through this."

"It's not me. I'm worried about him!" She was facing him again. "And I know you must talk to him. That's why I've told you about it. Just pull it out of him somehow, all right? Don't let him know I know about it."

"Virginia, he's going to know you told me. Christ, we've been talking for over an hour. What am I supposed to do? Just walk in there and ask him how the hunt is going? Just act like I had nothing else worth bringing up. Come on. You can see that won't work." Mike stood up and rested his arms on a white wooden fence. He grimaced as he got a splinter in his left hand.

"Here, let me get it." She held his hand with one hand and in no time had pulled out the splinter with the other. The sound of the back screen door slamming caused them both to look up at the house simultaneously. Virginia smiled happily at the sight of Bertha in her white uniform carrying a tray of lemonade out to them. Mike stared blankly at Virginia, not knowing what to think.

Upstairs, looking out at them through her bedroom window, Meg stood silently, sensing that somehow her prayers were being answered. This Mike Chandler down there talking with Virginia was going to bring her Kevin close to her again. She had watched him drift for weeks, watched him as he had anguished over what had happened, and now she felt a warm serenity fall over her. Things would soon be okay again.

Meg watched as Bertha carried the tray of lemonade over to Mike and Virginia and set it down on a small white table. Virginia introduced Mike to Bertha, who made just the slightest of curtseys before she finally, although timidly, grabbed Mike's outstretched hand with both of her own hands. Bertha's heart was so full of love, Meg thought to herself, and despite the painful bashfulness she initially experienced upon meeting a stranger, that outsider would very soon feel like a part of her. Meg knew that Bertha was truly a child of God.

She walked away from the window and over to her bed where she sat down and picked up a red leather bible Kevin had given her soon after her conversion, she opened it to one of her favorite passages. It was in Matthew, where Jesus told his followers not to worry. He told them they should not worry about tomorrow, that no one among them had added a single day to their life by worrying about tomorrow, and that they should not worry about food, shelter, or clothing. That surely God, who took such good care of the birds and animals, providing for all of their needs, that surely God would take care of their own needs. That worry would do absolutely no good at all.

This passage had saved Meg. She still remembered the first time she read it, how it had made such good sense, how she had not remembered reading it before, though she had gone to church all through childhood. As she thought back now to all she went through before she finally discovered the Lord, she smiled in satisfaction. She had gone through such a long period of pain and suffering, trying everything from yoga to psychoanalysis to antidepressants and nothing had worked. None of it had made her feel at peace with herself. Then, almost by accident, she had been staying at her father's house in Baltimore one weekend when Kevin had gone to Europe on business. She had watched the Hour of Power with Robert Schuller on TV with her Dad, who, although she didn't know it at the time, had just recently, after a lifetime as an atheist (as a good scientist should be), turned his life over to Christ. They watched the show that morning and heard Schuller talk about this particular passage in Matthew. She had asked her father if he had a Bible in the house, assuming that since he was watching the show it was a safe question, and he had given her a copy of the Possibility Thinkers Bible he had purchased through Schuller's telecast.

She had gone upstairs with it and read the entire book of Matthew. She had then, with no instruction or guidance, gotten down on her knees, closed her eyes, and prayed out loud. She prayed like she had never prayed before, with a great seriousness. She asked Christ to come into her life and run it for her, told him that she could no longer do it herself. Later that afternoon, as she flushed her Valiums and Seconals down the toilet in the upstairs bathroom, she felt happier and more at peace than she had felt in years.

Now, as she sat on the edge of her bed, reading the same passage that had started it all, she decided to get down on her knees again. This time she was going to pray just as seriously as she had prayed for herself in the beginning, though this time she was going to pray for Virginia, knowing that if it worked, Kevin would be happy.

Outside, Mike had just thanked Bertha for bringing the lemonade and was listening to her tell a story about Virginia's first lemonade stand, soon after they had moved to the ranch. "She was about, let's see, seven, yeah seven years old," she began, "and determined? Child was set. She was going to sell her lemonade from a cardboard box she had set up down by the road. Course, hardly be any cars up and down that road. So, her Daddy, he was real worried that no one be buyin' his little girl's lemonade. So he goes drivin' off, actin' like he had some kind of work to do, and he drives all the way into Cooper, and tells a few people about his daughter and her lemonade stand. Well, sure enough, pretty soon she be out there sellin' her lemonade to folks and she be hollerin up to the house for me to make some more." Mike had just entered Bertha's world.

After Bertha went back inside, Virginia said to Mike, "Come on, I want you to see my baby."

"Your baby?" Mike said, and immediately knew she meant her horse.

"Yea, I can't ride her yet because of the dizzy spells but I want you to see her. We'll get some treats out of the barn for her. Follow me."

Mike followed her into the barn and watched her as she moved over to an area containing a large storage barrel. She reached in and got a hand full of carrots. "Come on. You'll love her."

As they turned to leave Mike saw a strange looking elongated object lying over against the wall, wrapped in canvas and half covered with hay. "Your father collects torpedoes too?" he asked as he walked closer to the object.

"What do you mean?" Virginia was flushed with excitement over feeding her horse. "Let's go."

"I mean this. What do you suppose it is?" Mike asked.

"Maybe it's some kind of new farm implement Dad got. For the tractor. Who cares? Let's go." Without even getting close enough to recognize the object, she turned and raced out the barn door, carrots in hand.

Mike hadn't moved. He leaned down and pulled back a piece of the loosely wrapped canvas. He saw the bluish gray color of the pontoon and instantly knew what it was. Why would he have kept this? How would he have even recovered it? The waves must have washed it way to the north. Someone would have had to search the sea for days to even stand a chance of finding it. And why would he want it? Some kind of sick souvenir? "Jesus!" Mike exclaimed in disgust, before realizing that Virginia was waiting for him outside the barn. He covered it up with the canvas and threw a hand full of hay back on top of it before yelling to her, "Be right there." As he stood up and walked out of the barn he added, "You were right, just some kind of tractor attachment, I guess. Let's me see that horse of yours."

Just as they got to the stables, Mike heard Bertha calling for Virginia from the house. It turned out it was him she really needed. He had a phone call from a patient, a Mr. Cory. He could take it on the phone in the barn or back up at the house. He told Bertha he would take it in the barn and told Virginia he would meet her back in the stable area in just a few minutes. As he walked towards the barn he was so very glad that he had left this number for Richard. He had to talk to someone about what was going on. But could he talk to a patient about it? "Fuck it," he thought to himself. "I've gotta tell someone."

"Richard?" he said into the phone.

"Mike, I'm very sorry to call you but I just freaked when your receptionist said you were gone." Richard sounded fine.

"Yea, sorry about that. Listen, Richard. Are you up for a visit down here tomorrow, if I can swing it?" Mike spoke as he thought things through. He would tell Kevin he had to meet with a patient, an emergency. He would ask him if he could do it here rather than drive all the way back. It might work.

"Down where? I don't even know where you are," Richard said, perplexed.

"I'm down here in Virginia. Never mind. It was probably a bad idea. What's going on with you?"

"Oh, same old shit. Rebecca just can't get enough and I feel like her damn whore most of the time. What's going on with you?"

It occurred to Mike that someone might be listening in on their conversation from up at the house. "Richard, give me a number where I can reach you in about an hour."

"I'll be here until Rebecca gets back from the airport. She went to pick up her brother. Just flew in from Wyoming. Apparently in pretty bad shape. Possible nervous breakdown from what I can gather. Heh! Maybe a new customer for you?" Richard was in a good mood.

"Fuck that. I'm not taking any new patients." Mike thought for a second. "Listen, I'll call you back, all right?"

"Sure, that's fine. Talk to you soon." Richard hung up and Mike waited to see if he heard anyone else hang up a line from the house. All he got was a dial tone. No one had been listening.

He walked briskly towards the stables and only slowed down when he saw Virginia talking to her Dad while she fed her horse a carrot. "Shit," he mumbled to himself before approaching them.

"So," Kevin began, "I see progress all ready, Dr. Chandler."

"Pardon me?" Mike responded.

"With Virginia, she already seems a lot better. I am so very pleased that I called on you for help." Kevin stood smiling at his daughter.

"Yea, she's going to be just fine. But we have a lot of work to do." Mike paused. "But, that phone call, it was a patient of mine I must see, or at least talk to. Are you sure you want me to spend the night?"

"Arrangements have already been made. Bertha has your room ready and we eat at six-thirty." Kevin looked towards Mike as if to hear him accept the invitation.

"Of course," Mike began, "but I need to run into town for a few minutes. How far is Cooper?" He remembered the lemonade story from Bertha.

"Five minutes. Why, is there something I can get for you, something you need?" Kevin asked.

"Oh, no. I need to just make a quick run. Be back in thirty minutes. After all, if I'm going to be staying here for a few days I need to pick up some things in town."

This pleased Kevin and he left it alone, telling Mike which way to go down the main road to find Cooper. Kevin's attention turned back to Virginia as Mike waved goodbye to both of them and walked back up to the house. He passed Bertha in the foyer on his way out the front door and told her he'd be right back.

Once in his car he breathed a sigh of relief. "What the fuck?" he said out loud, frustrated with the recent turn of events. He started the car and pulled out of the driveway. He thought about the pontoon and could not come up with any possible reason why Kepler would have retrieved it and stored it in his barn. It occurred to him that perhaps it wasn't the same pontoon. But he knew it was. He had seen it up close. He had jumped into the ocean right next to it and pulled Virginia from the water. He knew it was the same one.

Once in Cooper, a small lazy town of about 5,000 people, he stopped at the first pay phone he saw and called Richard.

"Hello there." Richard answered the phone.

"You won't believe what I just stumbled across," Mike began.

"What's that?" Richard asked.

"Well, remember the story I told you about finding Virginia hanging on to what was left of a catamaran during the storm?" Mike had decided on the way into town that he needed to tell someone and Richard was the best person to tell.

"Yes, I remember," Richard responded.

"Well, I just found what was left of the pontoon hidden in her Dad's barn." There, he felt better.

"My, my. Now that is quite a find. What do you suppose it means?" Richard knew Mike was upset and reversed roles on him, briefly becoming the therapist.

"Jesus Christ, man. What do you suppose it fucking means? I have no idea but it's not exactly what I thought I'd run into down here."

"Just calm down." Richard tried to sound soothing. "Maybe it's not the same pontoon."

"Yea, sure. That's it. They just keep an extra pontoon lying around in the barn. Maybe for the horses, you think?" It felt great to be able to let go like this, and he knew Richard could take it.

"Now, now. You're getting all worked up."

"Richard, I know it's the same one. What I can't figure out is, number one, why would he have it, and number two, how did he get it? I mean, think about it. We left that thing floating out at sea. And, if you remember, there was a storm." Mike sounded exasperated.

"Have you considered that perhaps it was inadvertently towed in by the boat you were on? Tangled up in someone's unattended fishing line? You know you really haven't thought this thing through. Maybe that Captain Toby guy found it and gave it to her Dad. Why? Who knows? But it's not that far-fetched, now is it?" Richard sounded calm and was making good sense to Mike.

"You know, you might be right. But I need you to do me a favor. Remember that pub on Duke of Gloucester where we met for a beer last week?"

"Yea, I remember." Richard listened.

"It's part of a restaurant. Toby's restaurant."

"I know. You told me that the night we were there." Richard, knowing Mike's next thought said, "You want me to go ask Toby about the pontoon?"

"Yea." Then Mike thought about it. "I mean, no. Don't ask him. I will."

"You sure?" Richard asked.

"Yea, I'm sure." Mike had begun to calm down. He decided that he would find out later about it. For now, he wanted to believe the story. His thoughts became less frantic and he remembered Richard telling him about his girlfriend's brother coming to stay with them. "So, you're going to have a house guest. You okay with that?"

"Well, after all, it is her house. And it is her brother," Richard answered. "It does sound like he's in pretty bad shape. Convinced that someone is out to get him. Rebecca keeps telling him to stop worrying about it. We'll see how it goes when he gets here." Then, he added, "They should be back from the airport soon."

"Well, if you need some space. I suppose you could stay at my place while I'm down here. Nancy has a key at my office." Mike felt indebted to Richard for helping him get through this.

"I'll be fine here. If not, I'll call you," Richard responded. "Oh, and by the way. Are you planning on being back here by Saturday?"

"I don't know. Why?" Mike said.

"Well, Rebecca wants to go over to Rehoboth Beach for dinner on Saturday night. I don't know if her brother will be up for going out or not, but, either way, we're still going. Why don't you meet us there? It is about halfway back from where you are in Virginia, isn't it?"

Mike answered cautiously, "Am I coming as a guest? Or as a doctor?" He regretted asking this but he felt he had to know.

"As a guest of course. Remember, you're not taking any new fucking patients!" Richard laughed after he said this, trying to loosen Mike up a little bit more.

Mike didn't laugh back but be he did accept the invitation. "I'm sorry. I'd love to come." He paused, and then asked, "Where are you eating?"

"Not sure yet. Becca likes that Rusty Rudder place. I'll let you know more tomorrow. Give me a call," Richard answered.

"Will do," Mike said, "and thanks for hearing me out about all this." They said goodbye and hung up.

Mike drove back to the ranch feeling a lot better about everything. When he got back, the smell of Roast Beef permeated the house and he realized how hungry he was.

As Kevin had said, dinner was served at six-thirty. Virginia looked especially beautiful as she sat across the table from Mike and to the right of to her Dad. Meg was on his left and began by saying a long drawn out grace that everyone else simply seemed to endure. After they all said amen, Bertha brought in the food. There were new potatoes, green beans, and small round onions surrounding a Prime Rib Roast, served on a silver platter. Not much was said as they ate. Bertha waited in the kitchen at a small wooden table until she heard the sound of Kevin ringing a glass dinner bell, telling her that the main course was done and it was time to prepare coffee and desert.

Over coffee, Kevin seemed distracted, even pensive. He began to tell a story about a railroad in Zaire but soon drifted off into something else until finally the phone rang and he excused himself. Virginia motioned her finger towards Kevin's study and mouthed to Mike, "See what I mean?"

Meg excused herself and walked into the kitchen. Mike spoke to Virginia, "What do you mean?"

"See," she began, "he's starting up on this hunt thing again, he's obsessed with it." She looked slightly desperate but still ravishing.

"Virginia, he just went to answer the phone," Mike said to her.

"Oh, really? Watch what happens when he comes back in here." She sounded smug yet still nervous.

As soon as she said this they heard the door to the study open and Kevin walked back in to join them. He was smiling, almost beaming with delight. "What an excellent meal that was," he began, "and what a wonderful evening it has been." He said this last part almost as much to himself as to them.

"Yes," Mike responded, "it was a great dinner."

"Tomorrow, with any luck, we'll have pheasant," Kevin boasted.

"With any luck?" Mike inquired.

"Luck and skill," Kevin answered. "Say, Mike, do you love to hunt as much as I do?"

A short moment of silence passed as Mike looked at Virginia before answering. "Hunt? No, can't say I've tried it. But," Mike paused for effect, "I did do a fine job out the last time I went fishing?" Looking at Virginia and then at Kevin, Mike was sure this had been a very clever comeback, worthy of an appreciative laugh from Kevin.

Instead, Kevin replied softly, moving over to put his arms on Virginia's shoulders as he spoke, "Yes you did, Mike. You certainly did. And I am forever in your debt." Kevin paused and looked up at the elk head above the fireplace, continuing, "But to hunt, Mike. Hunting is my passion."

Mike looked at Virginia, who sort of grimaced as her father took his hands off her shoulders and folded them in front of his chest, still staring at the elk head on the wall. He stood there silently, mesmerized, smiling and lost in thought.

Mike stood up to say goodnight. He explained that he was exhausted from the drive down and wanted to be fresh for tomorrow. He went into the kitchen, thanked Bertha and Meg for the meal, and asked Bertha for directions to his bedroom. Virginia had quietly entered the kitchen behind him and spoke up, "I'll show him the way, Bertha. I think I'll get to bed too. Goodnight." She turned and walked out and Mike followed her. As they walked back through the living room, Kevin was gone. In the distance outside they heard the sound of his motorcycle and Virginia said to Mike, "His nightcap. Goes for a ride every night before bed."

Mike shrugged his shoulders, rubbed his eyes, and yawned. "Time for sleep. You look like you could use some almost as much as me." He followed Virginia up the stairs and to his room, where he said goodnight to her at the door.

Later that evening, once the house was quiet and everyone was asleep, no one heard a truck pull into the driveway and drive directly over to the barn. There it stopped and two men got out. They went inside the barn and came out carrying the pontoon, still wrapped in canvas. They secured it tightly to the back of the truck and drove away. In the house, everyone slept soundly, especially Kevin.

The next morning Mike woke up with a cool breeze blowing through the small crack he had left in the window next to his bed. He jumped up and closed the window before climbing back into bed, pulling the heavy quilt up to his chest. Today he would try something new with Virginia. He wanted her to remember the accident and all of the details. He would have to hypnotize her but he felt it was necessary.

She didn't remember much of what had happened She needed to deal with the grief of losing Nathan, or at least remember how it had happened. That was the first step in her road to improvement. Then she could start working on issues, talking things out, putting things in their proper perspective. He wasn't sure if he should try it without first asking for Kevin's permission. But, he decided that since Kevin had placed total confidence in him, it would be okay to proceed without mentioning it to him. After a quick shower he went downstairs, noticing that all of the other bedroom doors were open, the beds made. He was the last one up.

At breakfast on the patio with Virginia and Meg, he learned that Kevin had left earlier and would not return until evening. Mike asked Meg if he could use Kevin's study to work with Virginia and of course it would be just fine. Finishing their breakfast, Mike told Virginia to go sit in her Dad's study and try to relax as much as she could, that he would meet her there in ten minutes.

He went back upstairs and brushed his teeth. He sat down on the toilet, took a crap, and thought about how he would handle it if things got out of hand during the session. He knew that was possible. Although he had used hypnotism only a few times, it had always gone well. Now, as he washed his hands and combed his hair, he felt like he was doing the right thing. It would go well. Virginia wouldn't remember what she said while hypnotized, and he would know what he was dealing with. Confident, he walked downstairs to the study where she was waiting for him, staring out the window towards the vegetable garden, looking at her pumpkins on the lawn.

With little said before he began, he got her to fall into a trance very easily, even surprising himself with his technique. Beginning with a few basic test suggestions until he knew she was truly under, he moved on quickly to the issues he wanted to explore. "Virginia," he said, "tell me about the day you and Nathan went out on the catamaran."

She spoke steadily and with little emotion at first, "We knew there was a bad storm coming but it was hundreds of miles away, and it was such a beautiful day. We spent a few hours sailing and decided to head back in. The sky was getting cloudy and Nathan was worried about it. The sky grew darker and it started to rain really hard. The wind was too strong for the sail so Nathan decided to lower it for a while and said we would just hang on until it blew over."

"Then, after a while, we both knew it wasn't going to blow over any time soon. We knew we had to get back. Nathan raised the sail and we began to head towards the shore, or at least what we thought was towards the shore. I guess we were wrong. We had only been about three miles out earlier and now we realized we were heading in the wrong direction. Nathan turned us about and we tried to retrace our route. It was dark, rainy, and the wind was too much for Nathan to control."

"About then we saw a boat. A huge boat, one of those big party boats that holds a couple of hundred people. You could see some lights from inside the boat but the weather was too bad for anyone to be on deck. It was heading towards us and Nathan tried to stand up and yell to get someone's attention. But it was no use. The boat was rocking back and forth and the sea was lifting our cat up and down with the swells. No one would hear us. We watched as the boat got closer. Nathan couldn't control our boat so we just held on and waited, watching the ship get closer and closer. As we would rise up on a swell, we could see the interior lights from the ship clearly, even seeing activity inside. People partying and laughing inside the boat. I even think I heard some music before it was on top of us. And then it went right through us, tearing the catamaran into two pieces, leaving Nathan and I holding on to some netting, still rising and falling with the swells."

"Nathan had a cut over his left eye and it was bleeding. He talked to me and told me things would be just fine. All we had to do was hold on tight until the weather cleared. We wouldn't sink. The pontoon would float. We were safe. And then a piece of the broken mast came around with a blast of wind and hit him in the back of the head."

"I reached out and held on to him, but he was knocked out. He was very heavy and I couldn't hold him up. I tied some of the netting around his arm to hold him on to the pontoon. But on the next rise up the swell, his arm slipped out. When we came back down again he was gone. I held on tight like he had said to do. I was crying but holding on tightly. I remember slipping my legs through the openings in the netting, and then my right arm. And I held on to a small metal bracket attached to the side of the pontoon with my left hand. I waited. Every now and then I would look around and call out for Nathan but he was gone, and I would start crying again. After a while it seemed like the weather calmed and the swell went down. I remember it felt like I was floating, gently and effortlessly, and then I must have passed out."

"And shortly after that we found you," Mike said softly to himself.

Virginia's face expressed little emotion considering what she had just described, not uncommon with hypnotism. Mike smiled to himself, proud of his work, and brought her out of it.

"So, how did I do?" She asked, not remembering a thing.

"You did just fine, Virginia. Now we have a path to follow to get you better. And now I know what you went through. And I promise, you will be okay again. You will be as good as new, maybe even better, by the time we finish." Mike spoke with sincerity. Now that he had the details, he could gradually work the pieces in with the treatment. And she would be fine. "Heh," he said, "what do you say we take a break and go feed your horse some carrots?"

Virginia lit up with excitement as she exclaimed, "Yes!" This morning's session was over and Mike needed time to think about what he had just learned.

After lunch with Meg and Bertha in the kitchen, Virginia asked Mike if he thought they could take a walk and talk some more. Once out by the stables she looked up at him and he saw her eyes were filling with tears. He put his arm on her shoulder and turned her to face him, saying, "It's okay. Tell me what's wrong."

"I remember what happened from this morning." She paused and Mike swallowed hard, stunned that she remembered anything. He tried to brace himself for what might follow, as she continued. "Poor Nathan," she began to sob a little, "he tried so hard to help me but then he got hit in the head. I remember that part." Now she was crying and resting her head on his shoulders.

"See, this is what you need to do. Let it all out. He loved you and tried to help you, but he couldn't." Mike stopped for a moment before continuing. Deciding what he was about to tell her was okay, he continued. "But you know what? There is some good to come out of all this."

"Like what?" She looked up into his eyes.

"Like now you know it was an accident. A big party boat on its way back in. They just didn't see you out there. They probably never even thought to look for a small boat out there in that weather. They were just trying to get home."

"Yea, and that's good news?" She asked.

"Well, it will be good news when your Dad finds out that no one was intentionally trying to kill you. Didn't you say you thought he was out to get someone who was trying to hurt you? Now, if we tell him what we know, he'll see it was an accident and let it go." Mike saw her perk up a little.

"You're right. But I heard him talking and he sounded so sure. Oh, I wish I had never heard that conversation." She wasn't crying anymore. "Do you think we should tell him?"

"Of course we'll tell him," Mike said reassuringly.

"But what about the Mr. and Mrs. Hollingsworth? Someone was trying to hurt them. I heard Dad thanking Bill and Joe over the phone for watching over them and for getting the guys who broke into their place." Virginia had a startled look on her face.

"Probably just a random break in. You know, they were an older couple, had a nice place, very vulnerable. Some of these creeps look for situations like that to take advantage of. Probably just a coincidence that it happened right after your accident. But here's another good thing to come out of this. If you hadn't had the accident with Nathan, your Dad wouldn't have been suspicious, and he never would have asked Bill and Joe to keep an eye on the Hollingsworths, right?"

"I guess so, but it still gives me the creeps that Dad even thought someone might be trying to hurt us."

Virginia was serious now, wondering about her father's private life. "I mean, what could he have done to someone to make him even suspect that?"

"I don't know, but I can see you're already feeling better." Turning back towards the house, Mike saw the barn in the distance and thought about the pontoon he had found hidden there. He still couldn't figure that one out. "Heh," he said to her, "why don't you go freshen up and we'll take a ride into Cooper for some ice cream?"

Virginia smiled, wiped her eyes, and responded, "I'll be right back."

Once she was inside the house, Mike started walking towards the barn. He opened the barn door and the afternoon sun lit up the interior of the barn. He saw that the pontoon was gone, stood there dumbfounded for a few seconds, closed the barn door, and walked back towards the house to take Virginia out for ice cream.

CHAPTER 8

Cecil's plane from Cheyenne was scheduled to land at Baltimore-Washington International Airport on Friday afternoon. Laura had convinced him to go see his sister in Maryland because he simply couldn't function on his own for now and she knew he could afford the trip. She had come across a roll of thousand dollar bills in his bureau one morning while putting away the laundry she had done for him. She had wanted to ask him why he didn't have it in the bank, where it would be safe. She thought about helping herself to one or two bills but didn't. When she finally asked him about it, he told her he just hadn't gotten around to opening an account. "Leave five thousand in the drawer and put the rest in you own account for safe-keeping," he told her. "My wife had a huge policy. Most of the money is still in my bank account in Florida."

Cecil had seen Laura's doctor at Laramie General's Urgent Care facility the night before who had told him his condition would improve once he got through the grieving process. After all, losing your wife and kids like that would take a while to get over, and being in a brand new place all alone might not be the best medicine. He should be with a close friend or relative, if he had one. In one of his more lucid moments, Cecil convinced himself that the doctor was right. His new home would be there when he got back, and he was sure his big sister would keep him well out of harm's way.

He sat on the plane nervously chewing handfuls of peanuts and drinking ginger ale. Lucky for him, the seat next to him was empty so he didn't have to talk to anyone during the flight. He felt very confused. Why was he so screwed up? Things had been going so smoothly until he had moved in next door to Laura. The short road trip out west had been great. He didn't understand why he was falling apart. There were times now when he almost believed he really had lost his wife and children in a car accident. Laura and the doctor were right; he did need to be with his family.

As the plane landed at BWI, he was excited about seeing his sister. He had rarely seen her when she lived in New York City, only forty five minutes from his Long Island home, and now he was traveling two thousand miles to see her in Annapolis. Oh well, things are funny like that sometimes, he thought to himself.

He saw her as soon as he got off the plane and she looked great. His big sister, Rebecca, had always been there for him when he was a kid. He should have contacted her before he left town. She wouldn't have told anyone.

Once out of the airport parking lot and on to I-95, Rebecca looked over at Cecil and said, "No one has heard anything from your brother-in-law." Louis Fratino had dated Rebecca a few times after Cecil had married his sister, and he had stayed in touch with her. Nothing romantic had ever really developed between them. She had grown bored with all of the talk about race horses, but, every now and then he would call her just to say hello.

Cecil sat up straight on the passenger side as he said, "Shit. That's just great."

"Your wife has been calling and calling, first about you and now about Louis and I don't know what to say to her." Rebecca sounded surprisingly calm. "Think he's alright?"

"I don't know, Becca," Cecil responded, "I just don't know." Cecil thought to himself that Louis had probably been scared away or eliminated by Kepler, but he did not want to alarm Rebecca so he kept quiet about it.

They didn't talk for a few minutes. Then Rebecca said, "I can't wait for you to meet Richard. You know, you briefly talked to him on the phone when you called. He's such a nice guy. And great in the sack too, I might add."

"I almost wish you wouldn't discuss—" Cecil responded, thinking briefly about the motel clerk in

Indiana. Then he continued, "But I think it's great for you, Becca. So you are serious with this guy."

"I think so. He's different than the others. You'll see."

"Looking forward to it," Cecil said as he stared out the window at what little scenery there was on this ugly stretch of Maryland highway. After about a half an hour they pulled into Rebecca's neighborhood and she pulled into her condo community and parked in the carport.

When they walked in Richard greeted Cecil warmly, "Hello Cecil." His first impression of Cecil was not what he had expected. He seemed fine, not the nervous wreck he had pictured. "So," he continued, "how was your flight?"

"It was great, thanks for asking." Cecil was holding his blue calfskin suitcases.

"Here," Richard offered, "let me take those to your room."

"Thanks, just show me the way and I'll take care of it." Cecil was also surprised to find this guy Richard not at all what he had pictured.

After putting his bags away and washing his face, Cecil came out to join Richard and Rebecca in the kitchen. "Real nice place, Becca. What's for dinner? I am starving." Then, before she could respond, he exclaimed, "I know. I want crabs. Maryland Blue Crabs!" Cecil seemed very excited.

"Yes," Richard said, not really being a big fan of the local crab houses, "they do have an abundance of crab-shacks here!"

"So," Cecil asked them, "what do you say?"

Rebecca answered, "Well, Richard doesn't particularly enjoy all of the loud hammering that goes on there."

"That's half the fun," Cecil said, "but that's okay. I'm your guest, wherever you say, and it's on me." Cecil wasn't sounding or acting like someone on the verge of a breakdown. He acted like he didn't have a care in the world. Maybe the doctor was right, he thought to himself, all he really needed was to be around family.

They settled on a seafood restaurant downtown on Duke of Gloucester, near the traffic circle. Dinner was wonderful and Cecil had a wonderful time with the tiny wooden hammer and utensils that were provided to pry the meat out of the blue crab shells and claws. Richard and Rebecca shared a seafood pasta dish while they were both entertained watching Cecil try to find more crab meat with his small utensils. The hammering on the shells was a little noisy but they both laughed about it.

After coffee, lots of small talk, and a primer from Richard on out of body experiences, Cecil began to grow uneasy again. He wondered if his hammering had attracted anyone else's attention. The same feelings he thought he had left behind in Wyoming were back again. He thought he saw Kepler dressed as one of the waiters, serving a table across the room, looking back at him, winking. He rubbed his hands into his face and looked again. It wasn't Kepler.

"Say guys, this has been great. What do you say we get out of here? I'm bushed." Cecil feigned a yawn as he reached into his jacket and pulled out a wad of bills and decided that this would be his last public appearance for a while. He would just stay at the condo, where he would be safe.

Richard looked at the money and then at Rebecca, who didn't seem the least bit concerned with it. Cecil had always carried around a lot of cash and always paid for everything. "Okay, little brother, you do look really tired. I'm just glad you're feeling so much better."

"I do have one thing I'd like to bring up," Richard offered.

"Of course," said Rebecca. Cecil counted out the bills for the waiter, nodding in the affirmative to Richard as he counted out the money.

"I have a good friend, actually he's more than a friend, he is my therapist. If we can arrange it, I'd like for us all to have dinner together Saturday night over in Rehoboth Beach. If that's okay with you, Cecil. He's inviting a few of his friends and Rehoboth is a good halfway point from where he's staying in Virginia." This was the first Rebecca had heard of his plan and while she was usually up for anything, she paused to look over at Cecil before replying. Cecil looked like he was following what Richard had said but wasn't responding.

"Sure," Cecil answered, "that sounds great. Heh! What do you say we get out of here?" He stood up and stretched, then added, "Crab was excellent." He was trying now to act as natural as possible, but inside, he felt like he was starting to fall apart all over again.

Once back home, Cecil told Rebecca and Richard he was ready for bed. Rebecca reminded him that the key to the pool and jacuzzi were hanging on a key rack on the kitchen wall in case he felt like taking a dip. Once in his room, he felt better. He looked at himself in the mirror and even thought he looked better. But he did decide to get his hair dyed to a nice, light brown color, and maybe even cut a lot shorter, as soon as possible.

As he began to unpack his suitcases and put his clothes away in the chest of drawers, he thought of his wife, Kathy. He thought about how bad she must feel with him just leaving like that. But, she was a strong woman. She would get through it. He just felt bad about it for a moment, and when he saw he had remembered to pack his bathing suit he instantly felt better. It was one of his favorite suits; it was white, with small red and blue stripes on the side. He always felt like he looked good in this suit.

He looked at his watch and it was late. His sister had told him the pool was available 24 hours a day but he was tired. He thought about calling Laura in Laramie but decided against it. As he unpacked his pajamas, he yawned, knowing he would sleep well tonight, and he did.

The next morning when he woke up it was past ten. He walked out of his room, still wearing his pajamas, and walked to the bathroom. Not hearing any other sounds in the house, he assumed Richard and Rebecca had gotten up earlier and had chosen to let him sleep in. After a good warm shower he felt great, deciding he would definitely try out the pool later today, and also deciding at the same time that he would pass on the invitation to have dinner with Richard's friend that night. He just wanted to relax and not see anyone.

He got dressed and thought about taking himself out for breakfast, but his new resolve to go nowhere for a while kept him from leaving the house. He walked into the kitchen and opened the refrigerator. Seeing eggs, yellow cheese, and an onion, he decided to make himself an omelet.

Just as he was finishing, Richard and Rebecca came back in with a small bag of groceries. Richard spoke first, "So, Cecil, what do you say, still up for tonight?"

Without any hesitation Cecil responded, "No, Richard, I think I'm just going to kick back, take a swim, maybe a jacuzzi. Afterwards, order a pizza, maybe a movie. You guys go and have fun." He sounded like his mind was made up so they didn't even try to talk him into going.

"If you're sure that's okay," Rebecca said.

"I'm sure. Go, have a good time. I'll be fine." Cecil seemed genuinely relaxed.

"Well," Rebecca continued, "we were planning on leaving a little early and checking out some of the shops before dinner."

"That's fine," Cecil answered. "Don't worry about me." He stood up and started cleaning up his breakfast dishes.

"Here," Rebecca started, "let me get that."

"No, no, I've got it. But thank you." He leaned over and kissed his sister on the cheek. "I'm actually pretty good at taking care of myself nowadays." He smiled to himself as he began to dry the pan he had just washed.

"Well that's good to know," Rebecca added, before turning to address Richard. "Let's pack up, this guy doesn't need our help!"

Richard smiled back and said, "I'll be ready in a few minutes." Then, turning to Cecil, he added, "I do happen to know a good pizza place that delivers, if you're interested. And, if you want to rent a movie, I'll leave you my Blockbuster card." He reached for his wallet and took out the card, adding, "You're positive you want to stay here by yourself?"

Cecil turned to face them, almost shouting, smiling as he said, "Will you guys just stop it all ready, I'm fine. I want to stay here. Have a good time."

With that, Richard tossed the video card on to the kitchen counter, smiled back, and turned around to go get ready, saying over his shoulder to Cecil, "Then I guess we're out of here!"

Rebecca looked lovingly towards Richard and then back to Cecil, saying almost teasingly, "You bring your suit?" She knew how much he loved to swim.

"Of course I brought my suit," Cecil paused. "Now you go get ready and have a good time. I'll see you in the morning. And," he added, "thanks for letting me stay with you, I really do appreciate it Becca."

Thirty minutes later they were gone and Cecil was poolside. The temperature was a little cooler than he had expected but the sun was still warm on his skin. The water was heated in the pool and it felt good when he dived in to swim a few laps. Once back out of the pool he was chilly for only a few minutes before the sun warmed him up again and he dived back in for a few more laps. He spent several hours repeating this ritual until the muscles in his legs were very tired from all the swimming before finally returning to the condo to order his pizza. He was feeling somewhat better about things and free of the uneasy feeling that had overcome him the night before at dinner.

As he waited for the pizza delivery, he took another quick shower, rinsing his favorite swimsuit of chlorine and hanging it to dry over the shower door. After putting on a pair of khaki pants and a purple knit shirt, he went out to the living room, grabbed the remote, and deposited his tired and even somewhat sun burnt body onto the sofa. Surfing through the channels, he was elated to find one of his favorite movies was coming on at five o'clock on TBS, an old movie he had first seen as a child and loved. It was *Journey to the Center of the Earth* starring Pat Boone and James Mason.

He was only into the first thirty minutes of the movie when he heard the pizza guy ring the buzzer at the gate. "This is great!" he said aloud to himself as he stood up to answer the buzzer, excited about the way his evening was unfolding. He looked outside the window and was surprised to see it was already getting dark. Fall, his favorite season was fast approaching. He buzzed the pizza guy into the complex and dropped back down into the sofa.

Just outside the gates of the complex, Bill and Joe had been waiting patiently for over an hour for the sun to go down. They had planned on going in after dark, but when they saw the pizza guy at the gate, Bill was the one who thought to ask him who the delivery was for. When

Joe told the pizza guy that he was Cecil Clemenzi from Unit 22, the driver grabbed the twenty out of Joe's hand, thanked him for the generous tip, got back into his car, and drove away.

II

Mike and Virginia were just pulling into the entrance of the ranch after having made the run to Cooper for ice cream. It was amazing to Mike how much better Virginia seemed to be doing. He had taken the top down on his MG before they left Cooper and she was loving it. On the drive back she had been singing along to the songs on the radio as her hair flew back in the wind. As he pulled into the driveway and parked the car, they both saw that Kevin's car was not back yet.

"You really think we should tell him?" Virginia asked Mike. "I mean, he may really appreciate it or he may just flip out."

"He needs to know that it was an accident, if you're sure he thinks otherwise," Mike said.

"All I know is what I heard. And he'll be furious if he knows I listened in on his conversation that night." Virginia smiled, continuing, "But I sure do feel a lot better, thanks to you."

Mike almost blushed, quickly opening his car door and changing the subject. "You know, we still need to spend some time together to get you back to 100%."

"I don't know," she said, grinning as she got out of the car on her side, "feeling pretty good right now. In fact, I think I'm even ready for a real ride." She looked over towards the stables and then back towards him.

""I don't think so. Not quite yet," Mike said. "Your Dad would just love it if you fell off your horse just hours after I hypnotized you. Which he also doesn't know about! Maybe tomorrow. We'll see how you feel."

"All right, you're the doctor. But, tomorrow, I ride!" Virginia exclaimed.

"And," Mike began, "tomorrow I will be heading back home for the weekend." He waited to see her reaction to this.

"What do you mean?" Virginia looked confused, "Dad said you were staying here for a while."

"Oh, I am," Mike said, "I'll be back on Sunday. Just need to meet some friends for dinner up in Rehoboth." Then, cautiously, he added, "I'd love to take you along for dinner but I don't think your father would approve."

Virginia paused, then said, "We could ask him."

"Yea, we could. If I were coming back here after dinner, but I'm not. I need to run over to Annapolis after dinner to take care of a few things. I was going to spend the night at my place, catch up on any messages, and drive back down here on Sunday." Mike told her. Then he said, "But I'd love to take you out to dinner on Sunday night if you think it would be okay with your Dad."

Virginia seemed disappointed as she started to walk away, saying, "Yea, I guess we could ask him."

Mike walked towards her, saying, "Virginia? What's wrong?"

"Nothing," she answered. Then she turned back towards him and smiled, adding, "Nothing at all." She seemed okay.

"You know when he gets back I need to talk with him about how you're doing, how things are going with us," Mike explained.

"I know," she responded. "Whenever he decides to come home." He had been gone all day. "Usually when he goes hunting he stops off for an early lunch and he's back long before now."

As she spoke, they both heard the sound of Kevin's car slowing down and pulling into the entrance. He pulled up next to Mike's car and got out, walked towards the front of his car and stared at it contentedly. He had just gotten it back yesterday from the dealership in Norfolk. The body work from where the deer had damaged his front grill and bumper was complete and you couldn't tell it had ever been repaired.

"Those guys did a hell of a good job, don't you think?" He turned towards Mike, waiting for a response. Not having any idea what he was talking about, Mike nodded his head affirmatively as he said, "Looks great." He watched as Kevin, dressed in old fatigues, walked back to the trunk of the car, opened it, and removed his shotgun bag. He then picked up the canvas satchel that held his catch and held it up in the air towards them, smiling and saying, "Our dinner!"

Mike had never gone hunting and knew very little about it, but he had never imagined one did it in a Jaguar. Maybe Kevin had just parked his car at some sort of hunting club and gone out in a jeep or something. Mike had no idea. But it did look odd seeing Kevin standing there in his camouflage fatigues, holding a shotgun bag in one hand and a satchel full of dead birds in the other. Kevin moved towards them, now smiling at Virginia. "So, how's my girl doing?" Then to Mike, "Any progress?"

"Oh, absolutely," Mike began, "we had a great session this morning and she's feeling much better. We were just talking about that when you drove up."

"Really." Kevin smiled at Mike and began walking towards the house. "That's great. Come on hon'," now addressing Virginia, "let's get these birds up to Bertha, here, you take 'em." He handed the bag to Virginia. "There, now run them on up to her and tell her there's even enough for her to have some tonight." He stopped and watched as Virginia took the bag and began walking towards the house. "We'll be right up." Then he turned back to face Mike.

"Progress is a good thing," he began, "and I'm very pleased." He put his arm on Mike's shoulder and began walking with him away from the house. "So, what kind of progress?"

"Well," Mike began nervously, "we found out what really happened out there to her and Nathan." He felt a lot better once that part was out. "We found out it was all just an accident. She remembered the boat that hit them. It was a large boat, almost like a ship. One of those big party boats out of Ocean City. The kind large groups rent out for parties at sea, you know. And this one was just coming back in bad weather and didn't see the catamaran and plowed right into them. And Nathan, he tried to help her but he got hit in the head with the mast." Mike was going way too fast and Kevin stopped him.

"Slow down, Mike. Slow down. She just remembered all this today?"

"Well," Mike explained timorously, "through hypnosis she did. I had to find out where to start things off and it worked out well. At first she was upset, but now?" He paused. "Wait until you talk to her now. She's much better."

"This is good Mike. I'm pleased," Kevin said, then added, "I knew you were the right man for the job."

Mike, relieved Kevin wasn't upset with him, said, "You know, Mr. Kepler, you've got one special girl there."

"I know that, Mike. That's why I want you to keep working with her. You're just what she needs right now, I just know it." Kevin removed his hand from Mike's shoulder. They were both standing next to the white fence overlooking the meadow where Mike and Virginia had first talked.

"And I'm very glad you feel that way, sir," Mike responded, feeling more at ease now.

"She wants to go to dinner with me tomorrow up in Rehoboth but I said no."

Kevin looked at Mike as he said softly, "Rehoboth?" He had a puzzled look on his face.

"Yes, I'm meeting some friends up there for dinner. Then I thought I'd run back over to my place in Annapolis and check on things. Be back here on Sunday," Mike answered.

"I see." Kevin paused. "Rehoboth Beach. I know the place well. Where are you dining?"

"Not sure yet, maybe the Rusty Rudder," Mike said.

"Good place, great lobster." Kevin turned away and looked out over the meadow. "Perhaps we could both join you."

Mike, stunned, replied, "That would be great. Actually, it would make her very happy, I'm sure." Then he added, "I think it's about an hour's drive?"

"About that. Depending on the bridge traffic." Kevin referred to the twenty three mile long Chesapeake Bay Bridge and Tunnel.

"Quite a bridge," Mike offered.

"Thing of beauty," Kevin responded, before turning back to look at Mike. "We'll firm things up in the morning." He then turned and looked back towards the house. "Think I'll get cleaned up before dinner."

Mike followed Kevin back towards the house in silence, only to be startled when Kevin turned around to face him and suddenly exclaimed, "Why don't we call your friend, the boat captain. What was his name? Toby? Perhaps he could join us. If you think it would be okay for Virginia, that is."

Mike replied, "I'm sure she'd be fine with it. It might even be somewhat therapeutic." He paused before saying, "I'll call him this evening. He owns a restaurant over in Annapolis, you know, but he might be fishing tomorrow. Great idea!" Mike looked forward to the idea of seeing Toby again.

"Good, you do that," Kevin said. "See you at dinner." They both walked towards the house and Kevin began telling Mike all about the joys of pheasant hunting.

Later that evening, after enjoying the dinner and eating too much, Mike called Toby and yes, he was leaving early in the morning to go fishing and yes, he could meet them back at the Rudder tomorrow night. And, he assured Mike, he was really looking forward to seeing the girl again. Mike then called Richard and let him know that his dinner party had grown in size, suggesting that, if Richard would like, Mike would call the Rudder to add three more to the reservation. Richard assured him that Rebecca would take care of it and told him how much he looked forward to meeting Kevin, Virginia, and Toby. The next morning Mike spoke with Kevin briefly before breakfast. He and Virginia would meet him there at five-thirty. Megan, who was packing for a weekend retreat in Virginia Beach with her church group, would not be going.

III

Cecil sat in the rear of *Ma Bell*. Beginning at his feet, and stretching across the floor of the helicopter, was a long object wrapped in canvas. His hands were tied behind his back and his head hurt from where Joe had struck him with the butt of his gun after he had objected to getting into the helicopter earlier. He had been knocked unconscious for a short time and didn't remember getting on or being tied up. His feet hurt for some reason and his left leg had begun to cramp.

He was relieved when he heard voices again as they approached the helicopter. When Joe started the engines and they actually began to rise up in the air, Cecil felt like he might throw up, but he didn't. The tall one, Bill, got out of his seat in the front and moved back towards Cecil. He was carrying a small backpack and threw it down at Cecil's feet before speaking. "Things you might be needing out there." Bill stared into Cecil's frightened eyes.

"Out where?" Cecil asked.

"Where we're taking you," Bill answered.

Cecil started to vomit a little but swallowed the regurgitation. He began to shake and asked Bill, "Can you at least untie me?"

"Of course." Bill reached behind Cecil with a knife and cut the rope. "Go ahead, stand up, take a stretch or two. You need to get loosened up for your swim." Bill then reached down and opened up the backpack, showing Cecil several items he would be taking along with him. A flashlight, a bottle of water, a Snickers bar wrapped in plastic, and a small pocketknife.

"What's that stuff for?" Cecil asked as he stood up and stretched, watching Bill reach into the backpack and remove his favorite white bathing suit with the colored stripes he had last seen hanging on Rebecca's shower door.

"A shot at survival. The major insisted you be treated fairly." Bill then threw the swimsuit into Cecils's hands. "Here, put this on."

"He wanted me to wear a suit?" Cecil's hands shook as he held the swimsuit.

"No," Bill began to answer him, looking up towards Joe at the controls, who was turning back to them and smiling. "That was really Joe's idea." Bill paused before moving back to the front to take his seat next to Joe, turning only once more towards Cecil and yelling, "Now put the damn thing on!"

As Cecil took off his pants and began to put the suit on, the helicopter lunged to the right and he fell into the wall, hurting his shoulder a little. Cecil got the suit on and stood staring out the small window at the earth below. They were crossing over the Chesapeake Bay and the lights from Annapolis were beginning to fade. The dark shadows of the Eastern Shore loomed in front of them and the ocean was only about sixty miles away. Cecil felt cold. Sitting back down again, he began to examine the items from the backpack. The flashlight was a good one, and waterproof. The small knife was actually a Swiss Army knife, which he held just briefly in a threatening way as though he were going to use the blade for a weapon. He folded it back up and looked at the Snickers bar, realized how hungry he was but forced himself to save it for later. Finally, he looked across the floor at the long cigar shaped object wrapped in canvas and wondered what it could possibly be.

IV

It was about seven o'clock and Mike had just finished his lobster. Kevin and Virginia sat across from him, Richard and Rebecca at his side, and Toby at the end of the table. The food had been excellent and even though Kevin and Virginia had arrived late, they got there just in time to order with the rest of them. Most of the talk during dinner had been about the food and now that they were all just finishing, Kevin, who had ordered a bottle of champagne during the meal, was standing up and proposing a toast.

"To you Toby, and to you Mike, my eternal gratitude for saving my little girl." He smiled down at Virginia and continued, "And to life. For being such a wonderful and challenging game for us all to play."

"That's kind of a funny thing to say, isn't it?" Rebecca, now working on her third seven and seven, said loudly.

Kevin looked down at her and responded with a measured tone of pleasure, "Oh no, not at all. You see, life has been good to me, though it has been difficult. And when a victory comes my way, I drown for a time in the joy it brings me, or miss the joy of it happening at all."

Toby said to Rebecca, "I guess he told you." And the whole table roared with laughter. Mike looked across at Virginia and found her to be more beautiful than ever. Richard raised his glass to be the first one to respond to the toast. As the glasses all met and the laughter grew louder, the sound of *Ma Bell* passing over the restaurant went unnoticed. Unnoticed to all but Kevin, who gazed happily out the window overlooking the open sea.

V

About three miles out, Bill stood up and moved towards the rear of the cabin. He reached down and began to unwrap the pontoon. Cecil stared at it and clutched tightly to his backpack. He could tell they were descending and getting a lot closer to the water below. The sounds of the swishing, roaring blades was louder now as Bill reached down and grabbed the small metal handle on the side of the pontoon and unwrapped a small piece of netting that was left fastened to the side of the bluish colored missile. He pulled the pontoon easily across the floor of the cabin until he got it right next to the door. Setting it down, he slid the door open and a blast of cold salty wind came in. He looked back up towards Joe, who gave him a thumbs-up before descending even lower. Bill motioned for Cecil to stand up.

At first Cecil felt like he wouldn't be able to rise, but he did. He walked towards Bill and held on to a railing near the door, peering down into the dark ocean below. The sea was smooth with hardly any swell at all. Cecil looked at Bill and then back at the water about twenty feet below, just as Bill pulled the pontoon over to the door and pushed it out. Cecil watched as it hit the surface of the water and then looked back towards Bill. Knowing he had to jump now so he wouldn't lose the pontoon, he clutched tightly to the straps of his backpack as though it were a parachute, made a shaky sign of the cross, and with a swift push from Bill he was out the door and into the water.

The water was cold and very salty. However, the saltiness helped. Cecil was more buoyant than he thought he would be. He watched as the helicopter turned and headed inland and he caught a glimpse of the pontoon just a short distance away. He swam towards it. Although the backpack slowed him down, he reached it easily.

He struggled with it for a minute trying to figure out the best way of holding on, finally deciding to hang on to the rope netting with one hand and then tying the backpack to the small metal handle with the other. He tried unsuccessfully to mount the pontoon like a horse but he kept rolling over. He finally decided to just hang on to the handle and the rope. He began to realize how tired he was. He hung on tightly and started to swim towards shore.

On the distant horizon he saw some lights and realized how far out he was. His legs were already tired and he hadn't moved any closer to the shore. Perhaps he should rest first, he thought to himself. But he was so hungry. He thought of the Snickers bar and decided to eat it, thinking that it might give him strength in his swim to shore. Once he got out of this mess, he would never do anything bad again. He would change his life, he thought to himself as he reached for the candy bar. Maybe Kepler would figure he was dead, and that was fine with him. He would go back out to Wyoming and get his money from Laura. Then he would head for California. He took a bite from the Snickers bar, decided to save the rest for later, and quickly reached for the water bottle. Why had Kepler given him a snack? And the water? Did he really want him to make it back? Cecil took a drink from the bottle and put it and the candy bar back into the backpack. He urinated into his suit. Then he began to swim again.

After fifteen minutes he was exhausted. Trying to pull the pontoon and the backpack with it was too much. He should have just left it there and started swimming towards the shore without it. But he couldn't bring himself to leave it. What if he got too tired? He would need the pontoon. And the backpack.

He stopped to rest. He finished the Snickers and realized that half the water was gone. He reached inside the backpack for the flashlight. Maybe he could signal a plane with it. Then he took out the Swiss Army knife and stuffed it into his swimsuit. He shined the flashlight across the surface of the dark water until its beam faded out and turned to black about a hundred feet away. He shined it up towards the sky with the same effect. Oh well, he thought hopefully, a plane might still see it. Especially if he waved it back and forth, which he began to do, even though there was no plane in sight.

But the light was visible from below him. And the light drew the shark towards Cecil's frantically kicking legs. As Cecil looked out towards the horizon he thought about what his new life in California would be like. He would go to Disneyland whenever he wanted to. Maybe he could find a simple job managing one of those beach city mobile home parks in Orange County, or maybe San Diego. He would have to put up with the illegals, but that was a good thing too. It would be the perfect spot for him to blend in, inconspicuously. He would create a new identity for himself, he thought, smiling as he kept waving the flashlight at an empty sky. He might even have an orange tree or an avocado tree in a tiny side yard next to his trailer. He would grow old and be happy. He would become a good person.

E P I L O G U E

The tangerines were withered and dying on the tree in his backyard and the foggy gray sky, known as the June Gloom in Orange County, California, still gripped the skies above Huntington Beach, well into the Fourth of July weekend of 2010. Cecil hobbled out to pick up the old fruit that had already fallen to the ground. His left leg ended at the knee and his stump was wrapped in a red bandanna. It was his own special Fourth of July tribute that went well with his white polo shirt and cut off blue jeans. For twenty five years he had been walking on one leg and a crutch and he had it mastered.

He was finally leaving Orange County and looked forward to his trip back to Maryland to see his sister. He was also looking forward to seeing the White House again in Washington D.C., maybe even catching a glimpse of Obama. He wished he could do something to show his support for the president but he couldn't come up with any good ideas. Perhaps he could just stand, or lean, against the fence that surrounded the White House and if he saw Obama come outside he could just yell, "Thank you, sir!"

2010 had been a rough year so far for Obama. Some of the "toxic assets" from 2008 had resurfaced in the late spring, causing more problems for the banking system. The unemployment rate had jumped to 11% and North Korea was still out of control, launching new test missiles every other week. Cecil was determined to help somehow, and if a visit to the nation's capital to show his support could make a difference, he would make the trip. Now that he would be living so close to Washington, he could go over every weekend if he wanted to.

He carried the rotting fruit in one hand and held the crutch tightly in the other as he made his way back inside the sliding glass door leading into the kitchen. He had been able to sell his house with a nice profit, only because he had bought it so many years ago. Most of his neighbors were upside down on their mortgage and could not sell. He sold it for several hundred thousand less than what he could have sold it for a few years earlier, but he still sold it for three times what he had paid for it in 1985. Staring at the fruit in his hand before he tossed it into a trash bag, he realized it would be the last time he would be picking it up. His plane left for Baltimore in a few hours.

He remembered his sister's home back in Annapolis as though he had just been there recently, but twenty-five years had passed since the night he had been abducted. When he had recently heard from Rebecca that Kepler was dead, he knew it was finally safe for him to return.

On the plane he was seated next to a young woman who was about twenty years old and fascinated by his missing leg. She was a premed student and interested in prosthetics, one of the few booming fields in the currently weak economy due to all of the amputees returning home from Afghanistan. Combat at 20,000 feet had proven to be more than the Marines had trained for at Pendleton, Lejeune, or Twentynine Palms. They had only succeeded in pushing the Taliban deeper into the mountains of Pakistan, losing limbs in the process from sniper fire and IEDs. On Obama's order, and with the tacit approval of the Pakistani government, our forces had followed the Taliban across the border into an extremely unstable combat zone, which had proven to be very profitable for the prosthetics industry. The girl's name was Maureen and she told Cecil all about the latest innovations in prosthetic legs. He told her he had tried one a few years ago and hated it.

Maureen reminded him of a time in his life when he still had his leg, a strong desire to work on Wall Street, and even his family. When he was still a student at NYU and seldom ruffled by anything. He had taken the emotionally broken person he had been in high school and transformed him into a force to be reckoned with. He thought back to his first anxious moments as an intern on the floor of the New York Commodities Exchange, when he looked out across the trading floor and just knew he was going to be successful and make so much money. Maureen's drive and determination about her career in prosthetics brought back all of those old memories.

"So Cecil, are you married? Do you have any children?" Maureen asked.

"No. No wife, no kids. But I do have a sister," he answered, not even considering his wife, Kathy, he had abandoned so many years ago.

"Is your sister meeting you at the airport?" Then, displaying no pity towards him, she added, "Is she your only family?"

"Yes." He paused and looked out the window as he continued, "My only family." Then, looking directly at her he said, "And you? Big family?"

"Huge."

"Of course," Cecil paused before saying, "and they must be very proud of you."

"Oh yea, they are. But they can be a real pain at times. Seems like I can never really be alone, even in my dorm, my roommate won't leave me alone." Maureen slowly massaged one of her hands against the other in her lap and yawned.

"How different we both are from each other," he suggested, adding, "I can go for weeks without talking to a soul."

Maureen leaned back in her seat and closed her eyes as she said, "How truly wonderful that must be." A short time later she dozed off and said no more.

The rest of the trip was uneventful. The landing was a good one and the smiling flight attendant walked directly towards Cecil carrying his crutches as the pilot announced they would be deplaning shortly. Cecil was the first one off the plane. He noticed that some of the other travelers stared at him and he comforted himself by thinking that a few of them probably assumed he had lost his leg serving his country.

BWI airport was crowded with holiday travelers but he was still able to spot his sister, Rebecca, waiting at the baggage claim and as he greeted her he marveled at how good she still looked. On the way out through the automatic doors to the parking garage he noticed two men who quickly turned the other way when he glanced at them, as though they did not want to be recognized. He shrugged it off and followed Rebecca to her car. As they pulled out of the parking garage and followed the signs to I-95 he never turned around to look behind them, where he would have noticed an ivory colored Escalade following their car.

The trip back to Rebecca's condo in Annapolis took about an hour because of the traffic, but Cecil enjoyed being able to see the Maryland countryside he had not seen in so long. As they pulled into her parking lot, got out of the car, and began to walk towards the front door, the Escalade slowly drove past the entrance, as though they were also simply heading home. The tinted windows would have kept anyone from recognizing the two men in the vehicle. Bill and Joe had promised Kevin Kepler that if and when Clemenzi ever did return to Maryland, they would follow his instructions. His recent death had not commuted that order. In fact, his death had made it even more imperative that Bill and Joe comply with his instructions.

Later in the afternoon Rebecca and Cecil made plans for dinner out to celebrate Independence Day. Cecil wanted Maryland Blue Crabs and Rebecca told him about a new place she was sure he would love. Rebecca and Richard used to go there before he had divorced her for a younger woman. Rebecca thought back to the last time she had watched her brother eat crabs and realized it had been twenty five years ago, and how she and Richard had laughed watching him attack the crab claws with that silly wooden hammer.

As they drove towards downtown Annapolis and were just approaching a red light, the Escalade pulled up beside them and quickly pulled in front of them. Joe jumped out and rushed to the passenger side of Rebecca's car before Cecil even had time to think about locking it. Joe put Cecil into the front seat of the Escalade next to Bill, Rebecca into the back seat, and tossed Cecil's crutches into the rear of the SUV. He then moved her car to a side street and parked it before returning to the Escalade.

"Why?" Cecil spoke to Bill. "After all this time, why?"

"Mr. Kepler wanted you to see something," Bill responded.

"See what?" Rebecca responded bitterly from the backseat. Bill didn't answer her and nothing else was said for a long time as they began crossing the Bay Bridge towards the Eastern Shore.

About 100 miles southeast of their location, just a few miles off of Highway 50, was the home of Virginia Chandler. Losing her father had been the most difficult thing she had ever gone through, even worse than watching Nathan die in the ocean twenty five years earlier.

She had just finished helping her fourteen year old daughter with her Biology homework at the kitchen table and was now ready to spend some time with her husband, Mike. It was still early in the evening and they always took a walk before dark in the summertime. Their home outside of Salisbury had been a wedding gift from her father twenty years ago. It was a beautiful white two-story colonial with a veranda that stretched across the front of the house. The grounds took up a little more than three acres. Virginia and Mike took the same path every evening, which was a about a one mile walk through lush vegetation that circled around her expansive vegetable garden before leading back up to the house.

The sunset was still over an hour away as they began their walk and she held Mike's hand, as she always did when they first started off, only to drop it after the first few hundred feet as the rhythm of their footsteps on the dirt path began to give her a sense of peace. They talked about the day and how much their younger daughter was looking forward to the fireworks that night. Mike told Virginia a little about a new patient he had seen the day before, and how he hoped their evening would not be interrupted by a call from him. The new patient had been very depressed and Mike had given him his cell phone number, just in case. As they came around the final leg of the path and walked towards the circular drive in front of the house, the sight of the ivory colored Escalade in their driveway caused Virginia to exclaim, "It's Bill and Joe!" as she began to run towards the SUV.

Cecil began to tremble as he saw Virginia approaching the vehicle while Rebecca sat in the back seat, angry and silent. Bill got out first and greeted Virginia. Cecil heard her call him Uncle Bill as he held her tight. He wasn't completely sure who this woman was but it was becoming clear to him that she was probably Kepler's daughter. And they had brought him to see her. But why? To apologize? To make amends?

Cecil began to feel light-headed and somewhat disoriented. He watched as Bill and Virginia, and the other man, her husband he supposed, had a short conversation before he saw Virginia reach for her cell phone and apparently send a text. It must have been to her daughter because a minute later the front door of the house opened and her daughter came running out to greet Bill. So this was Kepler's granddaughter, Cecil realized. He watched as the little family reunion in the driveway finally ended with Bill saying goodbye to them and getting back into the car. At that point Joe got out of the car and hugged Virginia and her daughter and then shook hands with her husband before getting back in. They waved goodbye as the SUV turned slowly around the circular drive and headed out to the main road.

"So that's what became of his daughter. Everything worked out for her, after a few years of nightmares and a minor breakdown." Bill turned to look at Cecil as he continued, "And now, you have one more ride to take."

"Does she know it was me?" Cecil asked nervously as they were pulling away.

"She knows, why, you wanna go back and tell her you're sorry about everything?" Bill shot back at him.

"Actually, I was thinking I should probably do that." Cecil was squirming in the leather passenger seat.

"Apologize for what?" Rebecca asked.

Cecil turned around and looked at her and his eyes began to tear up as he spoke. "A long time ago I did a very bad thing."

"What kind of bad thing?" Rebecca asked.

"I paid to have her killed because I was so upset with her father. She didn't die, but her fiancé did, and her father made it his life's work to get back at me." He paused and looked at Bill in the driver's seat. "These guys already tried to put me away once so I guess they get to try again."

"But what about me? I didn't have anything to do with any of this!" Rebecca was starting to panic now.

"I don't know the answer to that Becca." Cecil looked at his sister in the backseat. "I just don't know."

He then turned back to Bill. "What about her? Can't you just let her go?"

Bill looked at the darkened sky along the road back towards Highway 50. "And where exactly would she go?"

Cecil knew this meant no as he turned back to Rebecca and said, "I am so sorry." His missing leg began to itch and he scratched the stump. Staring into the darkness ahead he saw a sign leading to the highway as they drove east towards the ocean. Occasionally, he saw fireworks in the distant sky.

When they got to Ocean City and took an exit towards the marinas, Bill turned to face Cecil again, saying, "So, you see this place coming up? This is where they first brought her back in from the boat after she was rescued. Then she went to the hospital. She was just a kid, you know." Cecil listened carefully, not sure what was going to happen next.

Bill pulled into the marina entrance and drove towards the water as he continued talking. "We weren't sure if she would make it at first but she was strong. Her father asked us to find you if you ever came back here and we did. He wanted you to see his daughter and we made that happen. He wanted you to have a chance to apologize and you had that. He wanted you to feel some of the pain his daughter must have felt. And then, against our advice, he wanted to forgive you for what you did." Bill pulled up in front of a group of catamarans that were docked close to the pier before he turned to Cecil again. "And this is where you get out."

Cecil looked at Rebecca, then quickly back to Bill. "Get out?"

"Yea, just open the door and get out," Bill said to Cecil. He turned to Joe in the back seat and saw he was helping Rebecca get out of the vehicle with one hand and reaching for Cecil's crutches with the other.

"Here you go," said Joe as he gently nudged Cecil with a crutch. Joe got out of the back door of the SUV and watched Cecil struggle to climb out of the front passenger seat. Then he jumped into the front seat next to Bill without saying a word and stared at Cecil's pathetic figure through the tinted window, wishing all of this could have ended much differently.

Cecil and Rebecca watched in disbelief as the Escalade pulled away, both of them feeling the wind that had just picked up from across the inlet, aware for the first time that night they were going to be safe. The catamaran in front of them bounced up and down in the water with the wind, splashing warm salty water on to the dock at their feet, and in the distant sky they could see and hear the remnants of a Fourth of July celebration as it came to an end.

ABOUT THE AUTHOR

Frank Drury spent the early years of his career as a struggling screenwriter in California before moving to the East Coast and finding success in the high risk world of futures trading, which is where he gained the inspiration for this work of fiction. He currently lives in Highlands Ranch, Colorado with his wife and daughter and continues to write fiction.

This book is available through Amazon.com or BarnesandNoble.com. It may also be ordered through your local independent book store. You may contact the author at frankdrury@gmail.com

Made in the USA
Lexington, KY
19 May 2011